1971

MONEY WRITES!

MONEY WRITES!

BY

UPTON SINCLAIR

Author of
" THE JUNGLE," " OIL !" ETC.

LONDON

T. WERNER LAURIE LTD.

24 & 26 WATER LANE, E.C.4

Republished, 1970
Scholarly Press, 22929 Industrial Drive East
St. Clair Shores, Michigan 48080

Library of Congress Catalog Card Number: 71-115274
Standard Book Number 403-00294-X

This edition is printed on a high-quality,
acid-free paper that meets specification
requirements for fine book paper referred
to as "300-year" paper

First published in England, 1931

PRINTED IN GREAT BRITAIN BY
NORTHUMBERLAND PRESS LIMITED, NEWCASTLE-UPON-TYNE

CONTENTS

[7]

CONTENTS

All my childhood and youth I heard a formula: " Money talks! " I never had any money, so to me the formula meant: " Shut up! "

Now the world has moved on, and talking is out of date. It is by means of the printed word that the modern world is controlled. So the formula must be altered: " Money writes! "

This book is a study of American literature from the economic point of view. It takes our living writers, and turns their pockets inside out, asking: " Where did you get it? " and " What did you do for it? " It is not a polite book, but it is an honest book, and it is needed.

It concludes a series, begun ten years ago, including " The Profits of Religion," " The Brass Check," " The Goose-step," " The Goslings," and " Mammonart."

ROMAN HOLIDAY

A NOVEL

By UPTON SINCLAIR

Crown 8vo.   7s. 6d. net.

America since the World War—the Roman republic after the destruction of Carthage—how much alike were they? History repeats itself; Luke Faber, the hero of this unusual tale, swings back and forth between the two civilizations, and cannot be sure which is real and which is dream. Strikes and labour revolts, "red" conspiracies and deportations, farm problems, speculations and hard times, feminism, divorce and prohibition—is it Rome or is it America? A poignant love-story and a cutting social satire are woven into the pattern of this new-old adventure.

T. WERNER LAURIE LTD.

CHAPTER I

CHRYSOTROPISM

Seventeen years ago I visited the marine biological laboratory of the University of California, and one of the world's greatest scientists explained to me his efforts at artificial fertilization. It was Jacques Loeb's thesis that all life is a chemical reaction; and to illustrate, he would take you to a little aquarium in which were swimming a number of tiny black creatures, the larvæ of the sea-urchin. The scientist would take a vial of salts and pour a few drops into the water, and instantly all the creatures would turn as one and swim towards the light. " That," said Loeb, " is what we call a ' tropism,' an impulse to move in a certain direction. In this case it is a ' heliotropism,' an impulse to move towards light. If we could enter the minds of those creatures, we should find that each is experiencing an emotion, each thinks that some reason of an important personal nature impels him to behave as he does. But science knows what has happened, the chemistry of the creature's cells has been altered. Some day—and not so far off—we shall understand human tropisms in this way, and be able to change by chemical agents the thing we call human nature."

I am writing upon the fifteenth of January, 1927, by the shore of that same ocean where the great scientist ventured his prophecy. The waters of this ocean are witnessing a singular event. It has been a damp and chilly day, and I look out over the sea from my study window, and the sunlight is failing, and a cold fog drifting in. The

[9]

temperature of the water is fifty-seven degrees; and having been in for a few minutes during the day, I know that these few suffice. Yet a hundred and three human beings, men and women, have chosen this day and night for an attempt to swim from Catalina island to the mainland, a distance of twenty-two miles at its shortest. The best time in which such a swim can be made is fourteen hours; and the radio tells me that all but a few of the contestants are falling out, many with bad cases of cramp, a few in delirium. Some will be injured for life; it may happen that one or more will lose their lives. A singular tropism to have seized upon a swarm of human urchins!

The answer is known to all readers of newspapers. Our leading California millionaire, purveyor of chewing-gum to the human race, had the idea a few years back to purchase Catalina island and turn it into a pleasure resort. This millionaire, having made his money by advertising, understands that in our great play-nation the one industry which is advertised free of charge is sport; a swimming race across the channel will bring millions of dollars' worth of publicity, and so he offers a prize of twenty-five thousand dollars. He might have the race in midsummer, when it would be a pleasure; but this would defeat his purpose—to proclaim to the world that from his island it is possible to go swimming in January. Therefore he sets this date, and pours a few drops of tincture of gold into the social aquarium, and a hundred and three human urchins, male and female, are seized by an impulse which Jacques Loeb would have called a " chrysotropism."

The arts of producing social tropisms have been enormously developed in modern civilization, but the developments are so recent that we do not realize them as yet. We are used to hearing about " mob emotions "; but the fact is, this stage of human life is gone for ever. No longer is the public permitted to originate its own tropisms, and run wild; the social mind now has masters. Shrewd gentlemen sit in swivel chairs and consult with subordinates as to what tropisms they desire to have created; and either these tropisms are created, or the masterful gentlemen find more competent subordinates.

These artificially created tropisms constitute everything really significant in present-day life. " World's series " tropisms and prize fight tropisms, evangelistic tropisms and moving picture tropisms, chewing-gum and safety razor tropisms, Harding-Coolidge tropisms, anti-German, anti-Russian, anti-Mexican tropisms—do you think I exaggerate in saying that such mass-emotions are now made to order, by means of so-and-so many gallons of tincture of gold?   Consider, for example, the ancient national antipathies; it used to be the case that these emotions had vitality enough to run themselves; but look at the urchins of France, how completely they were possessed, ten years ago, by an anti-German tropism, and how this has given place to anti-American, anti-British, and anti-Italian tropisms!   Any social chemist, knowing the formulas of the diplomatic tinctures, can explain to you that the French owners of iron have made a deal with the German owners of coal, and so have cancelled their orders for anti-German tropisms, and called instead for tropisms against American bankers and British oil concessionnaires and Italian traders in Tunis.

I am dealing in this book with a group of human urchins who hold themselves haughtily above the influence of social chemicals, the tropisms which move the vulgar herd. These lofty ones are the artists; my own tribe, the men and women of letters, who sit perched upon the apex of sophistication, and look with scorn upon all mass emotions. But observe the singular phenomenon—on approximately the same date several thousand men and women of letters retire to secluded corners to excogitate a thing described as " charm "; each cudgelling his or her head for some variety which can possibly be regarded as original; each delving into dusty tomes in libraries, looking up costumes and accessories, weapons, liquors and far-off, forgotten oaths; each sitting for hours a day pecking at a typewriter, with one eye on the clock and the other on the calendar.

Finally, on a certain date, several thousand men and women emerge from seclusion, each one carrying a manuscript of approximately the same size, and the same general style and spirit.

Is not this obviously a tropism?   And what has happened to cause it?   A magazine or publishing house has poured some drops of tincture of gold into the literary aquarium, and several thousand book-urchins have been seized by a simultaneous impulse to feel " romantic," and to put these feelings into a novel of from eighty to one hundred and fifty thousand words not later than May 1st, 1927.   In what way are these competing book-urchins different from the sea-urchins battling the waves in front of my home to-night?   I take up the local evening paper, and on the front page I find a cartoon, " Wonder What a Catalina Channel Swimmer Thinks About."   There are six little pictures, showing a swimmer in six postures of agonized effort; above the head of each is a legend, in larger and larger type, as follows : " 25,000 berries! 25,000 beans! 25,000 bones! 25,000 simoleons! 25,000 shekels! $25,000! "

Wonder what the writer of a $25,000 prize romantic novel thinks about!

CHAPTER II

FISHES AND PIKE

WHAT is the most important single fact about American civilization? The answer is: economic inequality. There has been inequality in other times and places; the poor have been equally poor, but never in history have the rich been so rich, or so secure in their riches, never have they built so elaborate a machine for flaunting their riches before the eyes of the poor. In this statement we put our finger upon the solar plexus of America: the land of a million rich engaged in devising new ways of exhibiting wealth; and of a hundred and twenty million poor, engaged in marvelling at the achievements of the wealth exhibitors.

There have been great empires prior to capitalist America; the number of them is buried under the sands of the ages. But we may safely make this assertion, that never in all history, or prehistory, has there been an empire in which the victims of exploitation were kept so continuously face to face with the evidences of their loss. Now, as ever, the poor are huddled in slums, far from the palaces of the rich; but now, for the first time, the rich have been vain enough—future times will say insane enough—to devise " Sunday supplements," " tabloids," and " home editions," to enable the poor to share imaginatively in the lives of the rich. The factory slave, having hung for an hour to a strap in a crowded street car, and eaten his tasteless supper of denatured foods, props his stockinged feet upon a chair, lights his rancid pipe, and spreads before his eyes a magic document—the twenty-four hour record of all the murders, adulteries, briberies, betrayals, drinking, gambling and general licentiousness of the exploiters of the world. It is all made as real as life to him—the palaces and shining motor-cars, the soft-skinned " darlings of luxury " in their ermines, and also in their lingerie; their elegantly groomed escorts in opera costume, and also in underdrawers—no intimate details are spared.

And then once a week the wage slave takes his wife and children to a moving picture palace, where they see people spend upon a supper-party more than a working-class family earns in a year. Old-time fairy-tales dealt with far-off things, but the modern movies deal with the instant hour, and why they do not lead to instant revolution is a problem that would puzzle a man from Mars. The explanation is the conviction, deeply rooted in the hearts of ninety-nine out of every hundred persons in the movie audience, that he or she is destined to climb out upon the faces of the other ninety-nine, and have a chance to spend money like those darlings of luxury upon the screen. It happened not so long ago that my wife was employing a high school boy of the working class, at the tasks of bury-ing the family garbage and scrubbing the kitchen floor. " The way the rich people drive their cars in this city is a crime," remarked this youth. " They don't pay any attention to the cops at all—they just go right through the traffic signals." " Well," said my wife, with mild irony, " you should report them. Such things ought not to be tolerated." " Oh, no," replied the boy, " I'm not worry-ing. When I grow up, I'm going to be rich, and I can do it too."

Do not suppose that this was an accident, the peculiarity of an individual youth. It is what had been taught to that youth in grammar school, in high school, in church, in the newspapers, the movies, and the political campaigns; the ethical code of a civilization, the propaganda whereby ten million youths are kept contented with their lot. Educators and moralists, editorial writers and Fourth of

July statesmen do not put it so crudely, of course; what they say is that America is the land of opportunity, and every child born in it has a chance to become president.

The Italian educator, Pestalozzi, tells how the little fishes complained of the voracity of the pike, and the pike held a conference, and adjudged the complaint to be justified, and ordained that every year thereafter two little fishes should be permitted to become pike. That most charming fable tells me all I need to know about the moral code of my country. For a million little fishes to be preyed upon by a hundred great pike is all right, because every little fish has an equal chance to become a pike—all he needs is to grow sharp enough teeth, and eat enough of the other little fishes. Any little fish that disputes the fairness of such an arrangement is a " sorehead," and his " grouch " is simply the expression of his conscious dental inferiority.

So now we can understand the " tropisms " which dominate the American soul. They are mass-impulses, having the intensity of frenzy, because they represent the aggregated terror of millions of little fishes, fleeing from the big pike, each jamming the others out of the way, each snapping at the next one's tail, as a means of evolving into pikehood. Each one suffers agonies of pain and fear, but has no time to feel sorry for himself, because he has been taught to believe that this is the proper and necessary mental condition for little fishes. " It's a great life if you don't weaken," he says; and is firmly persuaded of his destiny for pikehood, and rapt by the vision of the glory that awaits him. So you have the explanation of those hundred and three sea-urchins, swimming in the black waters in front of my home. Cold and exhaustion, rheumatism, drowning, broken heart valves, sharks, and the giant barracuda—all these " negative suggestions " each sea-urchin pushes away, and concentrates upon the faith that he or she will be a bit swifter or luckier than the others, and get first to the shore.

CHAPTER III

BEING SOMEBODY

Do not understand that it is merely the money; you will be crude and vulgar if you think that. It is what the money will buy—in other words, what the contrivers of mass-tropisms have created to give money its meaning and its grip. Two days have passed, and you can see the process in action with my sea-urchins. The race has been won by a seventeen-year-old lad, a " bell-hop " from Canada; and behold him lifted up into a golden cloud! His picture is in every edition of every newspaper in the land, and a hundred million people clamour his name; crowds besiege him, he is carried upon shoulders; contracts are spread before him, he has only to " sign on the dotted line," and he may travel about in private cars, and have managers and secretaries and press agents, and a glass tank, in which several times each day he swims in vaudeville houses before the eyes of thousands. All the rest of his life this glory will cling to him, he will be " somebody "; the very town where he was born shares in his reflected glory, he has " put it on the map."

One of the celebrities who ruled the world during my boyhood, the late John L. Sullivan, was introduced to Grover Cleveland, and wanted to put the latter at his ease. " A great man is a great man," said John L. " It doesn't matter if he's a prize-fighter or a president." And so every year America widens the categories of greatness, and takes new heroes into her Hall of Fame. The youth who swims the Catalina channel, the girl who swims the

English channel, the man who walks across the continent in forty-seven days, the man who drives a motor-car two hundred and seven miles an hour, the man who flies over the north pole, the man who eats a gallon of beans in eleven minutes, the girl who slays her rival with a hammer, the scientist who discovers a cosmic ray, the movie star who marries her seventeenth husband, the preacher who reads the Bible two hundred times—each one has his day, or perhaps his week or month, upon the front pages of the papers, each has his moving picture contract and his vaudeville " time," each his envelope in the " morgue " of the newspapers, where the clippings about him are indexed, and will be looked up whenever he comes to town, or does anything else that has " news value."

Strangers marvel at this clamour and lack of restraint, and think there must be some especial depravity in the American soul; but this is because our thinking about human society is still unscientific. " Vice and virtue are products like vinegar," said Voltaire; and every social manifestation has its cause. The cause of America's frenzy is simply the extremes of social contrast, greater than any to which human nature has hitherto been exposed. In order to understand the sea-urchins who swim channels, or the " human flies " who climb the outside of forty-story buildings, or the " walking stomachs " who eat twelve dozen oysters and forty-nine pancakes at a meal, it is necessary to have sympathy, and realize what it means to be a " nobody " in capitalist society—an obscure atom in a miserable mass, travelling in a crowded street car to a monotonous job, railed at by a nagging boss, wearing frayed clothing, eating dirty food, sleeping in a hall bed-room with the rent overdue. The victim of such conditions, driven to desperation, makes some hitherto unheard of effort, develops some hitherto unimaginable talent—and behold him suddenly transported into fairyland, riding in a limousine, carrying wads of greenbacks in every pocket, waited upon, flattered, caressed, loved, stared at, cheered, photographed, talked about. Does anybody wonder that

America is the land of unlimited possibilities, and that Japanese, Chinese, Hindus, Turks, Jews, Greeks, Italians, Poles, Papuans and Patagonians dream of emigrating to that movieland where every farm-house kitchen is a baronial hall and every drawing-room a cathedral?

All the way up and down the social scale, wherever you study these mob-excitements, you find the same artificially created tropism, the impulse to move in the direction of gold. The reporters who write up the sensational event, in a language which departs ever farther from English— each one is hoping to attract the attention of the " desk," and to rise upon the wings of this story to the permanence of " feature writing." The " desk " is hoping, by masterful handling of each new opportunity, to replace the managing editor in the affections of the publisher. The managing editor is hoping to avoid being replaced by a dozen too eager subordinates. The publisher is hoping to prove to some big banker that a newspaper is capable of affording its " eighty per cent. and safety," just the same as if it were chain grocery stores, or the diversion of industrial alcohol. From top to bottom the same " chrysotropism," the deadly pressure of competitive greed.

CHAPTER IV

THE SETTIN' DOWN JOB

FOOD, clothing, shelter, love, these are men's primary needs; and immediately after them comes entertainment. The slaves of the factory and the adding-machine must have a means of imaginative escape, and so we have a whole series of new tropisms, and a complex of industries exploiting them. Can you dance? Can you sing? Can you draw, or paint, or tell a story, or what have you? If you have anything, there is a nation-wide system for reproducing it a million times, and marketing it to all the world. Can you paint a pretty girl with rosy cheeks and flashing teeth, or a small boy with ragged pants and a bob-tailed dog? Any one of the popular magazines will pay you a thousand dollars, and two or three months later your painting will be on every news-stand in the United States and its dependencies. Can you make line or wash drawings of tall, aristocratic young heroes wearing new tailored suits or one-piece underwear? The advertising agencies stand ready to guarantee you a salary of six hundred a week.

Or can you make up little tunes? Do they come tripping through your head, accompanied by words in negro dialect, to the effect that I loves my honey and my honey loves me, and I's goin' to meet my honey by the old persimmon tree? I'll leave you to guess whether that is the latest " song hit," or something I just made up. For writing words like that, with little tunes to match, men are paid so much that they become indistinguishable from steel kings and master-bootleggers. They sell a million piano sheets, and two million phonograph records, and never while Broadway and Forty-second Street continue to intersect will men forget the story of Irving Berlin, Jewish street-rat and cabaret-singer, who won the love of the daughter of Clarence Mackay, lord of railroads and telegraphs, and high muckymuck of the Catholic aristocracy of the metropolis. The cold, proud father forbade the banns; and then said the lover—one tells the story in Broadway dialect, of course—" I love her and she will be mine in spite of you." Said the cold, proud father, " Suppose I cut her off without a cent? " Said the song-writer, with a languid smile, " In that case I suppose I'll have to give her a million or two myself." And so he did, perhaps; anyhow, they were married, and so great was the public excitement that reporters for the tabloids climbed up and peeked through the transom, and the happy pair had to flee to Paris, and sneak back by way of Canada.

Or can you tell stories? Then you are luckiest of all— the masters of world-tropisms will send their representatives to camp on your door-step. Consider my neighbour, Zane Grey. He cannot go walking without seeing his name on billboards, nor read the papers without seeing pictures of his sturdy heroes rescuing his lovely heroines. He grows tired of them—as I would if I were in his place; so he goes after big game fish, and having caught all there are in local waters, buys him a yacht and goes cruising to New Zealand—and what more could a steel king do?

Or Harold Bell Wright, who also lives out here in the wide open spaces, and is so rich—when a new one of his books is published, the pile touches the ceilings of all the drug-stores in Southern California. He has hotel and real estate subdivisions named after his heroines—in short, he is a classic right while he is alive. Or Peter B. Kyne— I have had the honour of watching him eat spaghetti in a San Francisco restaurant, and hearing him tell how the *Saturday Evening Post* had paid him twenty-five thousand dollars for his new story, and the Laskys had offered forty thousand for the picture rights—not counting book rights. and dramatization rights, and second serial rights, and foreign rights. Some of the screen writers and stars in Hollywood are making so much money that it's a bore taking care of it, and they engage regular business men to look after their investments, again just like the steel kings, and quite as it should be—why should not art be great, and the creators of beauty be looked up to?

When such quantities of tincture of gold are poured into the literary aquarium, is it any wonder that the swarm of book-urchins go quite mad, and crowd one another out of the tank, and bite off one another's tails? The jealousies of authors have been noted by all biographers and moralists, but so far as I know, the present work is the first in which the cause is set forth. The desperately competitive nature of authorship derives from the fact that the product can be reproduced without limit. When a man grows cabbages, he does not put all other cabbage-growers out of business; one cabbage is one cabbage, and there is no way to turn it into a million cabbages. But when Harold Bell Wright produces a book, it becomes a million books in a couple of months, and compels several hundred other authors to grow cabbages for a living. Therefore they hate Mr. Wright, and set up a clamour that his works are not great art, and that the ability to sell a million copies is not the final test of literature : a doctrine obviously inspired from Moscow, and intended to undermine the foundations of American culture.

Also, the occupation of writing is a dignified and agreeable one. The author lives at home, which pleases everybody but his wife. He can do his work in his own time, which means that he can play golf every afternoon, and so only the biggest bankers can afford to associate with him. Also he gets a lot of advertising, and so goes into " Who's Who," while his golf associates stand outside and peer wistfully over the fence. Also, in the hours when he does work, there is an impression that he doesn't work hard; the popular concept of an author's job is summed up in an incident that happened to my wife, standing by the garden gate, when a small urchin came along. " Have you got a job for me? " " What sort of a job? " " Well, I'll tell you, ma'am. The place where I work, they make me hustle too much, and what I'm lookin' for is a settin' down job."

There are in America two hundred thousand persons cherishing aspirations towards the " settin' down job " of authorship, and the high schools and colleges add ten thousand new recruits every year. I know with reasonable accuracy, because they send me their manuscripts and write me letters telling the story of their lives. Each candidate strives with feverish intensity for some new " line," some variety of " charm," some local colour that has never been exploited, some plot that has never been unravelled. And meantime, upon the watch-towers of several thousand newspapers, magazines, publishing houses and theatrical producing offices sit men with spyglasses watching for new talent, and when it appears, they grab it, and concentrate all the arts of civilization upon the task of coining it into the greatest possible number of dollars in the fewest possible number of days.

CHAPTER V

WHAT THE PUBLIC WANTS

THE theory upon which our greatest of all cultures has been built is that of a fair field and no favour, and the devil take the hindmost. We Americans have always believed in that, and up to date it has always seemed to work. But now, for some reason beyond our understanding, it appears that the devil is taking the foremost as well as the hindmost. We have seen during the last ten years an endless procession of plays on Broadway, illustrating the methods of committing every conceivable crime; we have watched the development of every possible variety of triangles, quadrilaterals and polygons, up to and including the last moments in the bedroom; we have become intimately acquainted with parricide, incest, sadism, and the whole index of " Psychopathia Sexualis." There is nothing left but the rarer and more obscure forms of abnormality; and so this winter we see the sensational success of three plays dealing with " Lesbian love," and drama courses in young ladies' finishing schools in New York now include an explanation of what this is and how it works, and it really has high cultural value, being history and psychology and æsthetics as well as drama, and the very latest thing—yes, old dear, they say it was a Russian ambassador's daughter who first made it fashionable in this country, and taught it to the daughter of a president, and he had to marry her off in a hurry.

The use of the arts in the glorification of depravity is covered by a formula: it is " What the Public Wants."

[23]

You hear that formula every ten minutes in the office of every yellow journal and tabloid in America; and likewise in the office of every popular magazine, and every producer of theatrical and cinema excrement. " Yes, I know, it's a piece of cheese, but it's what the public wants, and what can a fellow do? " The purpose of this book is to tell the " fellows " that their formula is twenty-five years out of date. It used to be a question of what the public wanted—until the science of psychology was put to practical use in the advertising business. Now, with " salesmanship " taught in several thousand schools, colleges and universities of commerce in the United States, every corner grocery has an expert who knows how to make the public want whatever he wants it to want. The presumptuous impulse of the public to do its own wanting is known to these ad. men as " sales resistance," and they lie awake at nights figuring ways to batter it to pieces. They have laid down so many advertising barrages that they have entirely destroyed the line which used to be drawn between necessities and luxuries, and now in America every man, woman and child has to have everything all the time. There is a week when everybody from Maine to Manila eats raisins, and a day when every red-blooded patriot takes home a box of candy to his mother, even though the old lady may have no teeth.

The ad. men all avow that what they unload on you must have " real value," otherwise their campaigns would come to nothing. They really believe this, because the professors of applied psychology have taught them that they have to believe it before they can make you believe it. They sing such things, and recite them in chorus, and dance their war-dances, and eat a million expensive luncheons every week at public expense. But stop and think for yourself, instead of for the benefit of those who live by emptying your pockets. What could be more silly than chewing-gum? Yet the whole world has to buy it, in order that our Catalina millionaire may have money to conduct swimming races to advertise chewing-gum.

What could be more uncomfortable than a starched collar?
Yet the collar manufacturers and the magazine publishers
have conspired against you to such effect that you cannot
succeed in business, nor even be happy in company, without
putting your neck into their white halter.

Or consider the thing called " style." Everybody who
wishes to be respected by his fellows has to throw away
his perfectly good clothes at least twice every year—and
for no reason that any living being can name except that the
clothing-makers may have the profit on the sale of a new
outfit. Or consider Christmas—could Satan in his most
malignant mood have devised a worse combination of graft
plus buncombe than the system whereby several hundred
million people get a billion or so of gifts for which they
have no use, and some thousands of shop-clerks die of
exhaustion while selling them, and every other child in the
Western world is made ill from overeating—all in the name
of the lowly Jesus? And yet so deadly is the boycott of
the Christmas grafters, that these few sentences would
suffice to bar this book from every big magazine and newspaper in America!

CHAPTER VI

THE MUCKRAKING ERA

THE theory that the public should have whatever ideas it wants, and that the test of what should be published is what will sell—that theory was tried out when I was a young man, and the world moves so fast nowadays that it is ancient history, and the younger generation of writers never heard of it, and will refuse to believe that it ever happened; if I assert that I lived through it, and saw it from the inside, they will say I have a subsidy from Moscow. Nevertheless, in the obstinate hope that truth will again some day be of interest to mankind, I will set down briefly the experience which bulked largest in my life as a would-be truth-teller; and which, incidentally, has determined the development of America for twenty years, and turned my sweet land of liberty into a paymaster of reaction throughout the world.

Twenty-five years ago the old anarchic idea of a free field and no favour prevailed throughout the American publishing business, and it occurred to a couple of bright young ad. men that the people might be interested in knowing how they were being robbed wholesale. They bought a derelict magazine from John Wanamaker, and made the try with Tom Lawson's *Frenzied Finance*. To use the ad. men's own slang, it was " a knockout "; the American people showed that more than any other thing in the entire world they wanted to read about how they were being robbed wholesale. One publisher after another leaped to the assault on the fortress of graft—there was a whirlwind of exposure, " the muckraking era," it was called, and for several years the writers made thousands of dollars, and the publishers made millions. It was no uncommon thing for a magazine to take on a hundred thousand new subscribers a month; and to us young enthusiasts of those lively days it seemed that the dragon of big business was going to devour himself.

But alas, a dragon does not swallow very much of his own tail before it begins to hurt. Big business rallied and organized itself, and the Wall Street banks got to work. You may read the details in " The Brass Check," if you are one of the few Americans who retain an interest in public affairs. Suffice it to say that every magazine in the United States that was publishing any statements injurious to big business was either bought up, or driven into bankruptcy, and " the muckraking era " passed into unwritten history. The public was told that it, the public, had become disgusted with the excesses of the muckrakers; and the public believed that, just as it had formerly believed the muckrakers. The public believes whatever it is told in print—what else can it believe? It was obvious enough that the " excesses " had been committed by those who made the muck, not by those who raked it; and the fact stands on record that out of the hundreds of exposures published, and hundreds of thousands of single facts stated, not one was ever disproved in a court of law.

Then came the war; and the manufacture of masstropisms, which had been a semi-criminal activity of bankers and big business men, became all at once the service of the Lord, carried on by the organized respectability of the country, with the whole power of the Federal government behind it. Just who was to blame for the world war is a question which will not be settled in our generation, if ever; but this much has become clear, history will not acquit any nation of guilt, and the diplomatic conspirators of France and Russia will carry the heaviest load. I am one of the hundred and ten million suckers who swallowed the hook of the British official propaganda, conducted by an eminent bourgeois novelist.

Meantime, here we were, the hundred and ten million suckers, doing everything we were officially told to do: eating rye bread instead of wheat, calling sauerkraut " liberty cabbage," saving our tinfoil and old newspapers, contributing to the Salvation Army, buying liberty bonds, listening to four-minute orators, singing " Over There," spying on our German neighbours, lynching the I.W.W. We sent a million men overseas, and they showed themselves heroes, and we who stayed at home showed ourselves the prize boobs of history, and taught our money-masters that there is literally nothing we cannot be made to believe.

Then came the Russian revolution, and gave our predatory classes the greatest shock of their lives. Before that, a Socialist had been a long-haired dreamer to be smiled at good-naturedly. The present writer, a queer, excitable youth who had " aimed at the public's heart and by accident hit it in the stomach," had even been permitted to publish two Socialist articles in *Collier's Weekly*. But now all that was ended over-night. A Socialist became a bloody bandit, who wanted to kill all the capitalists and nationalize all the women; the new arts of manufacturing tropisms were turned from the Germans to the Russians, and to-day, ten years later, there are patriotic societies, having millions of dollars to spend convincing the members of the Women's Christian Temperance Union that Jane Addams is a Soviet agent, and the child labour amendment to the Constitution a Moscow plot to undermine our young people. And don't think that I am just amusing myself with wild words; the earnest and credulous church people of this country are taught just exactly that, and by propaganda societies which big business maintains and pays for that job and no other.

So the doctrine of the open door in affairs of the mind was scrapped for ever, and tolerance and fair play were stowed away in the attic of American history. No longer does a big magazine of national circulation extend to a young writer the opportunity to explain how democracy may be applied to industrial affairs. There is to be no democracy for American labour, the " American plan " is another name for stoolpigeons and spies, blacklist and terror. Each individual steel-worker may bargain on equal terms with the most gigantic corporation in the world, and if he doesn't like the terms, he will be slugged, or thrown into the can, or if he is a foreigner, shipped back home to be shot by his native Fascisti.

And all over the world, America, which once went wild over Kossuth, now subsidizes defenders of " law and order " such as Kolchak and Denikin, Horthy, Mussolini and Rivera. Mr. Herbert Hoover's aide boasted in the *World's Work* how he starved out the revolution of the Hungarian workers; and Mr. Richard Washburn Child, ex-minister to Italy, and Fascist-in-chief to the *Saturday Evening Post*, tells his friends how Mussolini came to him to ask whether the American bankers would subsidize the march on Rome; they would, of course—and so we have a " stable government," which has crushed every vestige of modern thought in Italy. As I write, we are preparing to undermine the workers' government of Mexico, we are waging a war to keep our bankers in control of Nicaragua, and we are letting the British imperialists lead us blind-folded into a war to defend the right of their merchants to poison a hundred million Chinese with opium raised by the labour of famine-haunted Hindu peasants.

CHAPTER VII

THE EXCREMENTA OF TSARDOM

The reader will say: " You promised a book on present-day literature, and here you are back on the soap-box! " The answer is, I want to show the forces which make present-day literature the unwholesome thing that it is; and these forces are political and economic. You cannot understand a plant except you know the soil and climate in which it has grown; and if present-day American art is poisoned with pessimism, and if most of our leading young writers are drinking themselves to death, the reason is because they live in a world from which truth-telling and heroism have been banished by official decree, and there is nothing left but to jeer and die.

It is the great Fascist magazines and publishing houses of America, with their direct Wall Street control, which determine American literature and art; it is theirs to say who shall be great, famous, rich; and any young writer who defies them has his complete freedom to retire into a garret and starve. As I wrote twenty-four years ago, " The bourgeois garrets resemble the bourgeois excursion-steamers. They are never so crowded that there is not room for as many more as want to come on board; and any young author who imagines that he can bear to starve longer than the world can bear to let him starve, is welcome to try it."

I stroll on the beach where I am living, pondering this book, and now and then my mind wanders, and I discover myself repeating a list of names. It is something that rises to the surface of my consciousness several times every week, invariably the same names, and in the same order: *Harper's, Scribner's, Century, Atlantic, Leslie's, Cosmo-*

politan. What does it mean? It goes back thirty years in my life to the days when I was beginning to write; it is a list of the great magazines which then constituted my hopes of survival. Poor, pitiful youth, I stood as much chance of " landing " anything with one of those magazines as I stood of making a flight to the moon; but I continued to mail manuscripts to one after another—I kept a little notebook and sent each manuscript to the list of magazines, and checked them off one after another—that is why, thirty years later, the list runs through my mind, as invariable as the days of the week. I must have spent hundreds of hard-earned dollars on postage stamps, and the rejection slips I accumulated would have filled a trunk, save that I watered them with tears of vexation until they were reduced to a pulp.

One of the stories born of those days of torment is " A Captain of Industry "; rejected by forty or fifty magazines and publishing houses, and now one of the most popular stories in Russia, having been issued in scores of editions. I remember taking it to the Macmillans, and Mr. Brett was kind enough to let me see his reader's report. " What is the matter with Mr. Sinclair? " it began. I was tempted to answer, " The matter with Mr. Sinclair is that he hasn't had a decent meal for months." But one did not say things like that—not in those far-off days, when the second-worst of all offences was to be poor, and the worst was to let anybody know that you were poor.

The people of those days were interested in " manners." They shut themselves off in tiny social groups, selected upon the basis of similar incomes, and devised a set of minute differentiations of costume and behaviour, to distinguish themselves from all who were not members of their group. The most desirable groups, those who had the most money, developed the most fastidious manners, and were the most fussy—especially the ladies—about every detail. To try to get out of your group was called " climbing," and to fall from it was called " disgrace "; both were unpleasant, and the truly dignified behaviour was to stay " in that state of life to which it has pleased God to call you." That didn't leave much to write stories about, so the magazines of my boyhood were perishing of anæmia—the editor had to lie awake at nights worrying, for fear he might give offence to some maiden aunt, and cause her to withdraw her subscription, and speak unfavourably of the magazine to other maiden aunts at the church sewing-circle.

If you want to know what the literary world was like in those days, read Howells' " A Hazard of New Fortunes," which tells about a writer and his spouse who rose to the heroic effort of moving from Boston to New York; you will be thrilled by this " hazard," you will share the anxious tremblings of this most proper of young couples— such is the genius of Howells, which made him the darling of anxious, trembling young ladies, at that period in life where they took the great step which determined their social status for ever after.

When I was a youth, Howells was one of the great editors, and the best of them; he had " stood for " Stephen Crane, and I had the fond hope that he might " stand for " me. But alas, I did not come under the Howells' formula of " realism." The business of a writer was to show things as they actually were, never as they might be or ought to be; life was static, it was being, not becoming, suffering, not willing or doing. And this formula covered, not merely the novelist, but his characters; you might tell about men who got drunk and went to the devil, and about girls who were seduced and became prostitutes, and you would be in the best Russian tradition, and Mr. Howells would fight for you against the maiden aunts. But if you used your brains to find out what social forces caused men to become drunkards and girls to " go wrong "—if you even portrayed any character who used his brains to such a purpose—then you were banned by the formula, and the doors of the literary world were shut in your face.

This so-called " realism " of the Russian writers was the

spiritual reaction to Tsardom. The Russian did nothing but get drunk and consort with prostitutes for the very good reason that if they did anything else they were arrested by police agents and shipped in a convict caravan to Siberia; the reason why writers portrayed only drunkards and prostitutes was that if they portrayed anybody else, the censor would ban them, and if they defied the ban, they would join the convict caravan. The case of Dostoyevski tells the story—a young man full of hope and enthusiasm, they treated him to the nerve-shattering experience which you may read about in his " Memoirs of the House of the Dead." Whereupon he submitted himself to his holy masters, and wrote about nothing but prostitutes, drunkards, epileptics and religious mystics, and now the British bourgeoisie, impersonated by Arnold Bennett, hails him as the greatest of all novelists, so great, in fact, that it is a waste of time to mention anybody else.

The Tsardom with all its works is dead in Russia; that country is in the hands of new men, who believe that it is possible to act, and to bring about social changes by the human will. So the creative forces of art are released, and it is possible for Russian novelists to be interested in men who think and put their thoughts into action. It is only in Britain and America, where the money-masters still swing their lash, that critics gather the excrementa of Tsardom, and set them up on the altar of art to be worshipped as divine relics.

We think of America as a place of freedom and growth; and it is true that in the superficial things of life America changes like a kaleidoscope or a lunatic's dream; everybody has a new jazz tune every night, and a new model of car every year, and fashionable young people change their lovers as often. But when it comes to fundamental things, the inner spirit that really makes life and art, you find that America has become another " House of the Dead," where all things are fixed, and the Constitution and the Bible take the place of the Tsar's excrementa as objects of worship. The Constitution becomes " the greatest docu-

ment that ever emanated from the brain of man," and
our capitalist press had devised a tropism whereby several
millions of school children make speeches in praise of it,
and the one who praises most blindly gets a vaudeville
contract or something of the sort. The Bible is the
inspired Word of God, and any teacher of biology who
subtracts a jot or a tittle from it is arrested and fined, or
more mercifully turned out to starve.

And what is the purpose of this new idolatry? Simply
that the money-masters may keep the power to give orders
and be obeyed. Constitution-worship means that a group
of elderly corporation lawyers, known as a Supreme Court,
have power to make the law of the land anything the
corporations want it to be; the existing law they interpret
to suit the money-masters, and when the people protest
and pass new laws, they call these laws " unconstitutional,"
and the people believe it. Behind this regimen of the
dead hand, works the living fist of big business, collecting
from a pious and diligent working-class the heaviest tribute
that has ever been taken in any part of the earth at any
period of history. This fist is armoured with the clubs of
policemen and the rifles of militia, with the latest devices
in armoured cars and machine-guns and poison gas bombs.
Behind the fundamentalist cassock you find the strangling
power of ostracism, plus the blacksnake whip and the
lynching noose.

Such is Fascist America; and these masked forces con-
front the young writer, and say to him, with the utmost
politeness and amiability, write what we want written, and
we will heap upon you all the honours that your talents
deserve. The young writer, being for the most part guile-
less, and utterly untaught in public affairs, believes the
great statesmen and the great judges and the great editors
and the great preachers of his country. He lets them
take him into war to validate the loans of J. P. Morgan &
Company; and then, when he discovers how he has been
bunkoed, he takes to booze and motor-cars and jazz-parties
and the writing of " smart " conversation.

[34]

CHAPTER VIII

ARTIFICIAL SELECTION

My friend Mencken reads this manuscript, and favours me with his expert opinion : " There is, in fact, only the very faintest desire among the literati that I know to write anything other than what they do write—and I probably know even more of them than you do." This makes me think of a conversation which I once had with a leading Republican statesman of New York; I happened to refer to the corruption of our courts, and the statesman corrected me with a smile : " No, our judges are not bought, they are selected." The distinction is one of manners, and marks a stage of culture; it applies to the arts, as well as to the judiciary, and I beg my friend Mencken not to think me so crude as to picture the writers of my country yearning to serve the cause of social justice, and brutally bribed into writing against it.

No, the system is more efficiently run. The masters of the tropisms have the shrewdest brains in the world to help them understand the literary temperament. They produce a social environment in which the sensitive young writer finds a hundred good reasons for respecting the sanctity of privilege, and a thousand for looking down upon crude and noisy malcontents. And then, very gently and deftly, the sheep are sorted from the goats; those who acquire the leisure-class manner are lifted up to prominence, while those who fail in the tests of gentility are put to selling insurance or digging the ground.

My friend Mencken is a man who fights hard for his

[35]

ideas. He has called me a " tub-thumper " and other lively names in the course of our public battles, and he will expect to receive as good as he has given. Therefore I am going to illustrate the process of artificial selection which goes on among authors, by telling my experiences with the editor of a certain highbrow monthly magazine with arsenical green covers. The editor of this magazine happens to know me, and being a human and kindly cuss, he is moved to ask me for contributions. I, being the same sort of cuss, think up an idea or two, and suggest them to my editor friend; and so I test the process of polite selection whereby our literature is kept in order.

I was asked to write something for the maiden issue. All right, I answered. I would write an article discussing the editor of the *American Mercury*, showing how his ignorance of economics made futile his thinking about the modern world. But this suggestion, for some reason, did not meet with editorial favour! A second time I was invited, and submitted a sketch of Jack London, which you may read as a chapter of " Mammonart." I will stake my reputation upon the statement that this article is full of meat, as interesting a study of a man of letters as the *American Mercury* has ever published. But it came back; and why? Because the life of Jack London happens to illustrate the devastating effects of alcohol upon genius. And don't think that is a joke. My friend Mencken wrote me : " This magazine is committed to the policy of the return of the American saloon." I tried to argue with him; surely it is the duty of a wise and tolerant editor to give both sides a hearing; if the side of the prohibitionists is weak, what better than to let them display their weakness? But Mencken answered that the question was one which did not permit of discussion; no discourtesy to John Barleycorn would be permitted to shock the sensitive readers of the *American Mercury*.

One day a vagrant idea wandered into my mind, and I wrote a little sketch of Edward MacDowell, as I had known him, as a student at Columbia University. This manuscript had no social implications—unless you count the inability of Nicholas Murray Butler to comprehend the phenomenon of genius. My friend Mencken was enraptured—" a most charming thing," and so for the first time, and the last, I obtained admission between the arsenical green covers. The article made such a hit that Mencken wrote more than once, inviting me to do a series of articles about the interesting people I had met during my life. But how could I do it, in the face of the prohibition against prohibition? The most interesting man I had ever known was George Sterling. I had known him for twenty-five years, and he had been a suitor for my wife's hand in the days before our marriage, so she also had known him intimately; between us we could tell the inner being of one of America's greatest poets, a most reserved and shy personality. But alas! it would be another sermon against John Barleycorn. Mencken replied by asking me to write about George without mentioning alcohol, which is funnier than Mencken could ever be brought to understand—Hamlet without the ghost would not be a circumstance to it.

So here you see a great editor in the process of " selecting " the writers of America, in the interest of the American saloon. Shall I be crude, and suggest that this editor is subsidized by the liquor interests? I have heard this said, and Mencken has heard it also, and the last time we met he cited it among the dishonesties of prohibition controversy. I have no doubt whatever that he told me the truth; he belongs, not among the judges who are bought, but among the judges who are " selected." He is of German descent and continental tastes; an old newspaper man, he has always had his cocktails, and always means to have them, and resents with personal fury the idea that anyone shall keep him from having them. It happens that gentlemen of wealth share this point of view, and, observing Mencken's ardour and ability, are moved to put up money to found a magazine for him, so that he may " select " writers who defend the American saloon, and eliminate writers who point out the destructive effects of alcohol upon genius. After this process of artificial selection has been going on for a sufficient length of time, my friend Mencken will look about him and observe that all the leading young writers of America are in favour of the return of the saloon, and he will cite that as a powerful argument in favour of his policy.

As to John Barleycorn, there are two opposing camps, and I could get financial backing for a magazine to fight Mencken. But when it comes to hereditary privilege, this is not the case; the holders of privilege constitute a solid phalanx for its defence in every field of human life. They mean to keep their privilege and to pass it on to their descendants; and they are thoroughly organized, and thoroughly conscious. Their programme, so far as concerns literature, may be put into one sentence—that all those writers who oppose privilege shall earn their livings by selling insurance or digging the ground.

Ever since the Bolshevik revolution, this programme has been deliberately willed and executed, as much so as the latest merger of railroads or the subsidizing of Fascism throughout the world. There are a dozen men commanding billion dollar resources, who meet in Wall Street offices and decide what American culture shall be, and create the propaganda machinery to make it exactly that. The little man whom they have chosen to run these United States for them was a classmate at college with one of the group, so they know him thoroughly; he has been an office boy to the rich for thirty years, carrying out the bidding of those special interests which subsidize the Republican machine of his state. Now his friend and counsellor, a member of the firm of J. P. Morgan & Company, travels down to Washington and makes suggestions; and he has the backing of Mr. Hoover, who has been a servant to millionaires all his life, and of old Mr. Mellon, who is so rich that no president could ever reject his advice. They have put a leading Republican politician in charge of our baseball, and another in charge of our movies, and three more in charge of our radio. They have got our news-papers so firmly in hand that out of several hundred Washington correspondents there is not one single man to prick the expanding bubble known as " the Strong Silent Man of the White House."

As to the question of which authors shall write and which shall sell insurance or dig the ground, this rests with the publishers of our great magazines; and for these mighty men there exists a little system of breakfasts and luncheons at the White House, and week-end trips upon the naval vessel which is used as a presidential yacht at public expense. These honours are extended in regular rote, and the mighty men go away thrilled and inspired, know-ing exactly what must next be done to keep the country in the right path. Don't forget that these same publishers all come to the Wall Street banking-houses when they need a few millions for their newest mergers. There are no independent magazines of big circulations left in America —they are all " chains " now, the Curtis chain and the Butterick chain and the Hearst chain and the Capper chain and the Medill-Patterson chain and the Crowell chain— all of them run exactly like the department stores and shoe-factory chains, upon the same principles of standardization and mass production. They know what they are going to want a year from now, and they order their stories as they order their trainloads of paper from the mills; they even order their writers, they will take a young genius and " make " him, exactly as Lasky or Paramount will turn a manicure girl with pretty pouting lips into a world-famous " star." And the result of all their activities you have just heard Mencken set forth: " There is, in fact, only the very faintest desire among the literati that I know to write anything other than what they do write."

CHAPTER IX

YOUNG AMERICA

THERE are several ways by which we might approach the subject of present-day art and its economic interpretation. The easiest for me, and probably the most entertaining for you, will be autobiographical. Let me show you the world upon which I first opened my literary eyes.

I am a youth of eighteen, just out of college. I have been carefully taught by several professors that to read a book less than fifty years old is an unworthy and degrading action, and consequently I have never done it. I carry around with me some little red volumes of Horace, with which I beguile my spare hours while collecting material for obituary notices for the *New York Evening Post*. All the rest of my life it will be possible for me to be patient with young literary tories, remembering the chain-mail suit of prejudice into which I was riveted by my professors of academic snobbery.

Somehow or other I fell from grace; there came into my hands a copy of Barrie's " Sentimental Tommy," and for the first time it dawned upon my young mind that works of genius might be appearing now. You cannot imagine the revolutionary nature of that idea, to one who had been taught that the roll of literary greatness was closed and sealed. I began to read modern books, and the little red volumes of Horace accumulated dust.

This literary world of my youth was dominated by a writer named Kipling, an Englishman, you may remember.[1] But now from Aden to Zululand and from Angora

[1] Here follows a page of criticism on Kipling which—in spite of protests from Mr. Upton Sinclair—respect for the English Libel Laws compels us to omit.—*Publishers.*

to Zanzibar, the flappers are crowding to the movie palaces to see Mary Pickford in " Little Annie Rooney," and coming out to bob their hair and cut short their skirts! And black boys and yellow boys joining the Young Communist League, and setting up a bust of Lenin instead of an idol in their huts! Swarming from a hundred different lands to the University of the East in Moscow, and preparing to take up the coloured man's burden, of compelling the white man to become a comrade instead of a killer!

Also there was a lady novelist whom everybody read, a truly advanced and intellectual lady who belonged to the very highest English society, and invited all America to come in with her. When a new book of hers was published, the stacks in the department stores looked like fortifications, and with every volume you got a premier free—no, not a premium, but a real live premier of the British Empire, with all his heart secrets, and how his political enemies tried to ruin him by making it appear that he had—well, you know what I mean, but it wasn't said in plain words, because young girls read Mrs. Humphry Ward.

We had American novelists also. There was our Richard Harding Davis, only he told about handsome young American engineers who went to Central America and put the spiggoties in their places, with the help of the American navy arriving gloriously in the last chapter to put down the bad revolutionists and put in the good ones, just as we are doing to-day in Nicaragua. Also Davis wrote the most perfectly lovely stories about a young society darling named Van Bibber, who solved all kinds of problems and set everything in the world right with the most wonderful grace; he thought nothing of knocking out three terrible thugs with one arm while holding his fainting lady love upon the other. The Van Bibber papers thrilled the readers of *Scribner's*, while *Harper's* featured Mrs. Ward, if I remember, and the *Century* specialized in another lady—what was her name, she wrote

" Little Lord Fauntleroy," and the best English society received her, and permitted her to tell us about their love-affairs.

Also there was Henry James, a *Scribner* writer, too, and I read every line of his thirty or forty novels; because I had come to realize that I must know what our ruling classes were like, and James was the man who would tell me. He had the most scrupulous regard for truth—he thought nothing of using up eight hundred pages to find out exactly what had happened in the way of a sexual intrigue between two of his characters twenty years ago, and to show you the writhings and twistings of the souls of these characters while the old guilty secret was coming out. For years I read these rather nasty scandals of the rich, and couldn't understand why it should be of such supreme importance whether she did or she didn't, whether he had or he hadn't. As with everything else in the modern world, it remained a mystery until I came to study economics, and realized that under the bourgeois law such old scandals determine property rights. It is upon property that bourgeois society is built, and it is property that decides whether people are worthy of having their scandals pried into and exposed by great geniuses like Mrs. Humphry Ward and Henry James.

CHAPTER X

EPISCOPAL THINKING

New writers arrived. There came Stephen Crane—and I did not read him, because they told me he was " bad." He wrote about a " girl of the streets," quite boldly and frankly, and that was against all the rules of literary America. Of course we knew there were " girls of the streets," you could not go for a walk in the evening without having half a dozen offer themselves at bargain prices; but if this were told about in novels, the moral scheme of the bourgeois world would be upset, for the ladies of refinement read novels, and it was to keep the ladies of refinement in ignorance about sex that the girls of the street were sold so cheaply—a great English historian, Lecky, had explained that to us in a passage of justly celebrated eloquence.

Then came Robert W. Chambers, and he was more clever than Crane, he was really naughty, but always sugared with a moral coating; his exquisite heroes and heroines would drink and gamble and dally with elegant temptation for a hundred thousand words, and then in a final thousand would be saved for virtue. The young ladies in boarding-schools thrilled at this delicious danger, and kept the latest Chambers novel under their pillows, and wrote him " mash " letters—I know, because it happened that the lady who is now my wife was then a pupil at a boarding-school on Fifth Avenue, one which boasted in its catalogue that the pupils had opportunities to meet the Goulds and the Vanderbilts; and one of the young ladies wrote to Mr. Chambers, telling him how she adored

[43]

his last hero; and there came in reply a note reading in substance as follows :

" DEAR MISS . . . ,—Do not have any admiration for my novels.   There is no sincerity in them.   I write for money.

" Yours truly,
" ROBERT W. CHAMBERS."

In those days I had no inside information, but I can understand now—Mr. Chambers was one of the victims of what was known as " the Collier set."   Robbie Collier was a fashionable young millionaire with a taste for litera-ture and politics in between his drinking bouts.   Young writers and illustrators would appear on the scene, and the generous Robbie would invite them to dinner and give them a contract with his magazine and a card to his country club; they would spend their afternoons sipping cocktails in the Hoffman House bar, and in a year or two would know nothing to write about but sports, motor-cars, women's dress and fashionable fornications.   I could name a dozen men to whom this happened; some of them died at fifty of congested livers, and others are living on in a fashion I am too charitable to describe.

Then came Winston Churchill, and the fortifications of his books in the department stores out-towered both Mr. Chambers and Mrs. Ward.   Mr. Churchill was an American gentleman of the old school; he wrote about America, and not about the Long Island smart set, and that was to the good.   If his novels were big and rather crude, that seemed all right, because he was writing about a big and crude country.   He started with the beginning of our history, and brought us forward to the present day, one novel every two years, as regular as an astronomical event.   Mr. Churchill talked about " democracy," and no doubt really thought he meant it; but he revealed that there was a propertied class in America, and this class governed, and somehow it always happened that Mr. Churchill's heroes and heroines belonged to that class.   In one case,

[44]

" The Crossing," if I remember, the theme required that the young hero be a pioneer, but somewhere in the story it was deftly conveyed to us that his ancestors had been real ladies and gentlemen, and so it became all right for him to marry the genteel and lovely heroine at the end.

We didn't have intelligence tests in those days, and lacked the convenient phrase, " mental ages." Among my papers I find a review which I wrote for a Socialist paper, discussing Mr. Churchill's novel for the year 1910, and I find myself complaining of the " intellectual and spiritual immaturity " of his work. He had got down to modern times by then, and his characters were riding in motor-cars and playing bridge and getting divorced. It was this last custom which troubled Mr. Churchill, and his novel, " A Modern Chronicle," was a tract on the new practice. I am going to quote my review because I can find no better way to tell you about Mr. Churchill's novels, and at the same time exhibit to you what passed for thinking among those Episcopal church circles in which both Mr. Churchill and myself were brought up.

" When you wish to write a novel dealing with divorce you have always one situation : a man or woman has in some way been led into an unworthy marriage, and later on in life the man or woman discovers the true soul-mate; and then what is to be done? The old solution was to have them renounce and suffer many agonies until the concluding chapter, when the novelist mercifully disposed of the superfluous member of the trio, leaving the hero and the heroine to live happy ever after. That is the solution of ' Jane Eyre '; and I remember how it thrilled me when I was a boy as old as the American people are now. I rather took it for granted that this would be Mr. Churchill's solution. As I went on, however, greatly to my surprise I discovered that the hero and the heroine were apparently going ahead to get a divorce in spite of everything; and I put the book down and stared about me, wondering if it could possibly be that Mr. Churchill was going to write a book in defence of divorce. He had made

his hero and heroine such very sensible people that it
seemed he was closing every other gate save that one.
However, I realized that this could not be the case, because
when the heroine went ahead to get the divorce Mr.
Churchill gave such a repellent picture of Reno, Nevada.
Of course, it is true that the people who go to Reno,
Nevada, and get divorces are many of them unpleasant
types; and doubtless the political judges who grant the
divorces are also unpleasant types. Apparently Mr.
Churchill does not realize that neither the hero nor the
heroine nor the demon divorce are to be blamed for this.
There is no reason why, if we are going to grant divorces
to New York people, we should not grant them in New
York; and there is no reason why we should assign the duty
of granting the divorces to vulgar political judges.

" I went on with the story and finally got to the solution
which Mr. Churchill has worked out. His heroine gets
her divorce, but against her conscience, so that she is
properly and respectably miserable afterwards, and marries
the hero and, of course, makes them both miserable. They
go to live in a narrow little New England town, and the
heroine insists on going to a respectable society church and
having her feelings hurt because nobody speaks to her.
She also makes the unfortunate husband angry by her
attitude, and when one of the insufferable pillars of the
respectable society church insults the hero, the heroine takes
the side of the pillar of the church. She makes her
husband so unhappy that he fills up his house with a
collection of disreputable Newport divorcees, and goes off
riding on a half-crazy horse and is killed.

" Apparently nobody is expected to perceive that all the
unhappiness which grows out of this divorce is owing to
the fact that the heroine gratuitously places herself at the
mercy of the opinions of the respectable bourgeoisie. You
feel this at the very moment where the divorce begins to
be talked about. The hero and the heroine have previously
been sensible American people, talking about things in
sensible ways; but when they begin to talk about divorce,

neither of them points out to the other any of the obvious facts which make the divorce and remarriage between them not only a perfectly proper thing, but even a social duty. Their conversation is confined to their blind craving for ' happiness,' and, of course, when we have met that word ' happiness ' a dozen or more times we understand that the blind craving is destined to lead them to destruction— since every seventeen-year-old moralist knows that the desire for happiness is a wicked thing which must under no circumstances be indulged. They never mention the fact that there are more intelligent people in other portions of the world, among whom they could perform work of social usefulness and importance. Instead of going abroad for a year or two as such a couple naturally would, they settle themselves in a town and proceed to let the town make them miserable. We are given to understand that among the Newport set with whom Mr. Churchill's novel deals there are only two classes of people—those who are horrified by the getting of the divorce, and those who have got divorced more or less frequently and have nothing else to do save to get drunk.

" Of course it would never do for Mr. Churchill to end the novel with the hero being brought home on a stretcher from his insane horse-back ride. There must be a happy ending. So away back at the beginning of the story we are made acquainted with a man who has worshipped the heroine from boyhood, who has been her friend and consoler in distress, and who has sternly rebuked her for getting the divorce and remarrying. This second hero now comes forward and the heroine is made blissfully happy in his arms. The absurdity of which conclusion is apparently not realized by Mr. Churchill. The divorced ex-husband is still alive, so the heroine's third marriage is under the baleful cloud of divorce quite as much as was the second one. Is the seventeen-year-old moralist to understand from Mr. Churchill that a divorce and one remarriage constitute a social crime, while a divorce and two remarriages constitute a happy ending? "

[47]

CHAPTER XI

SOCIAL ANTITOXINS

If a living organism is to survive, it must develop antitoxins against invading enemies. And so it happened with the social organism in the days of my youth; the bacteria of hypocrisy and greed were not permitted to devour it at will. A group of young writers came to the defence, and, for the reason I have already set forth, they were able to find an audience. I have told about them at some length in " Mammonart," and will here merely summarize briefly.

First, Frank Norris; I shall never forget the bewildered dismay with which I, the victim of many years of academic education, read that pioneer novel, " The Octopus." Was this a nightmare of a distorted mind, or could it possibly be that such things had happened in my land of the free and home of the brave? I decided that it couldn't be— the newspapers would surely have told me about it! I did not learn the full truth until twenty years later, when I met Ed Morrell, who had stood four years of solitary confinement for having tried to help the settlers of the San Joachin against the railroad " octopus." Meantime, Frank Norris had died young, and it was the happiest fate that could have befallen a muckraker. Three decades of heart-sickness and defeat are not to be wished upon any young artist; and still less would one care to see him reformed, a fat and well-groomed poodle in some large publishing establishment.

And then Jack London. In those early days the seeds

of decay that were in his character were not apparent to us; he came among us as a young god, a blond Nordic god with a halo about his head, and the voice he raised for the oppressed workers was a bugle-call. Lying on the campus of Princeton University, near which I lived, I used to read instalments of " The Sea Wolf " in the *Century*, and it is only a few times in life that we experience such thrills.

And David Graham Phillips. I lay a wreath upon the tomb of this noble-hearted, old-style American from the Middle West. In those young days snobbery was still a force against which a man could fight; it had not yet become the whole of civilization. How Phillips loathed the beautiful parasitic female, and how he lashed her, and her male provider, in those perfectly documented pictures of business and social graft! But alas, the parasitic female now has all the money to spend for novels, and she has raised up a school of secondary parasites, the literary lounge-lizards. I do not know how I can better sum up the change which has come over America in twenty years than to mention that these novels of David Graham Phillips were published one after another in the *Saturday Evening Post*. If their author were to come back to the gorgeous show-palace in which his publishers now dwell, he would not get by the detectives in the lobby.

He died at the height of his powers, shot by a man for what reason the public has never been told; he was buried, and his reputation was put into the same grave. It is nothing less than a conspiracy of our kept critics which deprives this magnificent talent of its influence. It is true that his work is unpolished—but will any kept critic assert that the work of Rousseau is polished, or that of Tolstoi? Phillips is one of the great moral forces of our literature, and he will come into his own, just as surely as the American people awaken from their dope-dream.

And then Edith Wharton. It is only rarely that a member of fashionable society takes to writing; they don't have to, and it seems hardly quite good form. But now and then one breaks the rules, and then the police reserves have to be called out to handle the mobs in the bookstores. In this case the writer was not merely a member of real " society," but an artist as well; never before had this happened in American history, and it was embarrassing for the kept critics. They couldn't call this lady a liar, as they did with the common plebeian muckrakers, who were under the necessity of writing for a living. Mrs. Wharton was admitted to know; and here she was declaring, in " The House of Mirth," that really rich and socially prominent people idled and drank and gambled, and that a young girl might be morally ruined while seeking to enhance her charms with fashionable clothes.

And then Robert Herrick. Here was another scandal; a supposed-to-be-respectable professor at Mr. Rockefeller's newly subsidized university, who presumably had opportunity to meet the " best " people, and who implied that a fashionable young architect might connive at the violation of building inspection laws, and that business men might hire him to do this; also that these business men were buying legislatures and judges. As time passes, all popular novelists come to deal with marriage; and here was Robert Herrick, actually suggesting that wealthy husbands and wives occasionally broke the seventh commandment! Underneath all his books, as of Mrs. Wharton's, ran the theme that when you became extremely rich, you did not necessarily become extremely happy. You can see how that meant the undermining of bourgeois idealism, and how necessary it became for those who control our cultural life to put up their money and buy out the magazines which were furnishing such reading matter to the masses of the people.

CHAPTER XII

LITERARY VIGILANTES

THE " muckraking era " culminated in the efforts of the
" progressives " to elect Theodore Roosevelt president in
1912. It wouldn't have done any good, because Roosevelt,
while he talked like a crusader, always acted as a
" practical man "—so he described himself in a letter to
Harriman, begging campaign funds from that super-
corruptionist. But the idealists gathered in convention,
and sang hymns and went out to battle for the Lord.
Their enemies laughed at them, for by that time every
great magazine that stood for the public welfare had been
either bought up or driven into bankruptcy, and there was
no longer any way to reach the great mass of the people;
there has not been from that day to this, and there never
will be again until the workers and farmers have united
to forge themselves a weapon of deliverance.

The world war came, and the idealism of America was
diverted into a new channel. The writers of America were
organized and drilled, along with the rest of the population; " Vigilantes," we called ourselves, and there are many
who would not enjoy having their antics recalled. Ten
years have passed, and one American writer here purposes,
as briefly as possible, to record his shame, and ask forgiveness from the thousands of young men he helped to
decoy into the slaughter-pit.

It was my task, self-assumed, to hold the radical movement in line for Woodrow Wilson's policies. Needless
to say, I never asked or received a cent from anyone, and

the little magazine which I edited and published cost me a deficit of six or eight thousand dollars for the ten months of its history. I am happy to say that I never swallowed the propaganda of our allies, and never ceased to warn our public against the perfidy of ruling class statesmen in Europe : so much so that the post office authorities refused entry to my magazine, and I only got by through a series of accidents—that my wife happened to have a United States senator for a cousin, and another for a next-door neighbour in girlhood; also that I had the fortune to have a telegram to Colonel House delivered to him while he was in session with President Wilson. My little paper was barred from England on request of the United States Naval Unintelligence; so you see, I do not have so much to confess as some of my fellow-vigilantes!

How could I have been trapped into supporting the war? I thought that Woodrow Wilson really meant his golden, glowing words; I thought he was in position to know what I couldn't know, and would take the obvious steps to protect us against diplomatic perfidy. I knew nothing of the pre-war intrigues of the French and Russian statesmen against Germany, which had made the war inevitable, and had been planned for that purpose; I knew nothing of the secret treaties which bound the allies for the war. When the time came for us to enter, I sent President Wilson a telegram, urging him to condition our entry upon the agreement that all territories taken from the Central Powers should be neutralized and placed under international guarantee. If that policy had been followed, the ghastly farce of Versailles would have been avoided; in fact we would never have entered the war, for the allied rascals would have been exposed, and forced to make peace by the public sentiment of their own peoples.

We went in; and the story-writers and poets and illustrators and actors and musicians of America were set to work to do their part in making the world safe for democracy. They wrote patriotic songs and red cross appeals, and spied on their foreign-born neighbours, and drew posters and made speeches selling liberty bonds, and went overseas and sang and danced for the boys. And while they were in the midst of it, the Bolsheviki broke into the strong-boxes of the Tsarist diplomats, and published to the world those secret treaties which showed our precious allies in a series of bargains to loot the world, in defiance of President Wilson's promises to the German people. And what did the literary vigilantes make of that? The answer is that very few of them knew anything about it, because the newspapers of America suppressed this most vital news of the whole war. Only the *New York Evening Post* published the treaties, and straightway it was driven to the wall, and purchased by a member of the House of Morgan. What the vigilantes chose to believe were the " Sisson documents," forgeries which the Russian reactionaries palmed off on an American editor who had turned amateur diplomat, and proved himself more silly than anything he ever printed in the *Cosmopolitan Magazine.*

My quarrel with Woodrow Wilson is not because he caused me to make a fool of myself, but because he fumbled the greatest opportunity that any statesman ever had in all history, and wasted the efforts of a whole generation of his countrymen. My reason for mentioning the subject here is to show the writers and artists of America what it means to them that all the sources of information and publicity of their country are held as the personal and private property of men whose activities have nothing to do with human welfare, but solely with the profits of their own predatory group. We Americans went into this hideous adventure, because the House of Morgan and its allied banks had backed the wrong horse, and stood to lose hundreds of millions of dollars. At any time in future that it becomes necessary for us to validate bonds held by the House of Morgan, we will go into a war with any nation whatsoever, big or little, Hayti or Nicaragua, Mexico, China, Japan, Russia, France or Great Britain; and when that time comes, the great chains of

[53]

newspapers and magazines and publishing houses and moving picture producers and exhibitors, all now tied up tight with the financial system, will see to it that you, the writers and artists of America, regard it as a war to make the world safe for democracy, and repeat all the antics you performed in 1917-1918: just as now they cause you, reading this statement of plain historic facts, to become indignant and call me harsh names.

CHAPTER XIII

RED VERSUS WHITE

I APOLOGIZE to you, my readers, for writing all this history. But a new age has come, and unless you know its economic bases, you cannot understand its literature and art. Have patience with me for just two paragraphs more, and we are done with politics for good.

The Russian revolution came. The greatest event in history, it has determined the past ten years, and will determine the thinking of mankind for the rest of my stay on earth, and yours. It was not merely the crash of a great empire; it was the fact that for the first time a revolution occurred in a country which had come to some extent under the modern forms of large-scale industry. It was revealed that in such a society the strongest single group is the organized machine workers. These workers, through their trade councils, took charge of Russia; and in so doing they gave us a sketch of history for the next hundred years. The cry, " All power to the Soviets," turned the politics, industry, science, literature and art of mankind into a struggle between two opposing forces, the newly awakening labour organizations, and the holders of privilege based upon paper titles to the means of production.

The new Soviet form of government was born amid the horrors of revolution and civil war; therefore it is a military thing, protected by a dictatorship. This makes it appear anti-democratic, whereas it aims at the widest democracy ever known. Needless to say, we have never had democracy in America; ever since the Civil War we have had plutocracy, maintained by the subsidizing of political parties and the purchase of legislatures and courts. Our democracy is a hope, for the most part feeble; and surely the Russians also have a right to hope—since they are applying the great principle to industry, the real power in the modern world, whereas we Americans are completely resigned to having our business affairs run by Henry Ford and Judge Gary and Rockefeller and Doheny and a few such masters. The democracy of the Soviets, a thing in the womb seeking to be born, and the democracy of Capitalism, matured into a flaunting prostitute—such are the two forces struggling for power, and their struggle conditions the thinking and writing of every author in the world.

I set aside books for later discussion; there are still independent publishing-houses, and a writer of books can, in the last extreme, beg or borrow the money and print his own writings. But books do not count for much; what rules the thinking of Americans are moving pictures, radio, and Sunday supplements and popular magazines which circulate by the millions every week and month. All these great capitalist institutions are now agencies of propaganda, and all writers who serve them are henchmen of big business, making war upon the new freedom in the interest of the old slavery. I do not mean to say that all such writers consciously produce anti-Bolshevik propaganda; many of them are just making America attractive, and distracting the masses with jazz and sex and luxury and fashion and crime and mystery and every conceivable form of futility. The individual writer or artist may have no idea what his work means; but rest assured that the masters of the pay-roll know, and select our cultural diet with care and definite purpose.

Meet my old comrade and fellow-worker, Joseph Medill Patterson. Twenty years ago Joe was the red hope of the radical movement, the author of that brilliant muckraking novel, " A Little Brother of the Rich," and of numerous labour plays which wrung your heart. Joe knew that his family had stolen from the public schools of Chicago the land upon which its great newspaper stood, and had bought several elections in order to hold its loot. But as time passed, the ties of blood asserted themselves, and Joe weakened in his rage against the criminal rich. He went to war, and learned the use of machine-guns and poison gas bombs, and now he has a store of them in the basement of the new white stone palace in which his great murder-newspaper is housed. Captain Patterson, ex-Comrade Joe, is now a master-Fascist; and he has not only the Chicago *Tribune*, but the *Daily News* of New York, the trashy tabloid with more than a million readers; also *Liberty*, the barber-shop weekly, upon which I am told he has lost several millions, but he does not mind, because it is a cause—the liberty of American big business to put fourteen million Mexicans into slavery. I happened to pick up a copy on Lincoln's birthday of this year, and I found an editorial calling for a new war with Mexico, and praising the last one as the best thing that had ever happened to Mexico; also a panegyric on Lincoln by a preacher—but you bet that preacher didn't quote what Lincoln had said concerning the Mexican war!

Meet the great Jesse L. Lasky, newspaper man, gold-miner, band-leader, magician-manager, and now lord of the moving-picture realm. Mr. Lasky has no military title, so let us call him Emperor of Orgies. The emperors of old knew only the orgies of their own time and place, but Mr. Lasky knows the orgies of all times and places, and at three weeks' notice will produce a set of the ruling class diversions of Persepolis or Paris, Nineveh or New York, Sodom or Chicago, Harnak or Hollywood. But when the Russian revolution came and threatened the orgy-enjoying rich, Mr. Lasky hastened to the rescue, to make the world safe for orgies. Who could better reveal the horrors of the nationalization of women in Russia, than one who knows so well the moving picturization of women in America? In the year 1919, at the height of our White

Terror, Mr. Lasky produced an elaborate feature-picture called "The World and Its Woman," with Geraldine Farrar, opera singer, and her husband, Lou Tellegen, as the stars, and it took my prize as the most hideous piece of hate-propaganda that had ever come under my eyes.

And how do you think Mr. Lasky got all the details about the blood-thirsty "reds"? Why, he hired an author who had lived among them—had actually been one of them, in fact. None other than my old friend Thompson Buchanan, volunteer publicity agent for the Paterson Pageant! That was fourteen years ago, when ten thousand silk-workers of Paterson, New Jersey, went on strike, and in those days we thought they were just poor devils, and it was a shame for the police to poke their batons into the abdomens of the pregnant women; we didn't realize that there were little Bolsheviks inside those abdomens! Some of us went out to make speeches for the poor devils, and get arrested with them; and as a means of overcoming the newspaper boycott, we got up the Paterson Pageant, and worked day and night over it, and bankrupted ourselves—how well I remember that agonized final meeting, when Mabel Dodge pledged her furniture to get the last five hundred dollars! And then the newspapers implied that somebody had robbed the strikers of the proceeds of the show!

Well, Thompson Buchanan was our publicity man, and worked like the wily Ulysses to outwit the capitalist press. And now here he is writing poison-propaganda for Lasky, and he can do it so easily—all he has to do is to turn everything upside down, portraying it exactly the opposite of what he knows it to be! The Tsarist aristocrats become beautiful and saintly and patriotic heroes; the peasants are well-fed and groomed like Hollywood stars, and love their masters and pray to God for their safety; while the Bolsheviks are monsters with twisted and distorted faces, who divide their time between murder and lust—just as Thompson Buchanan observed during his work with John Reed and Ernest Poole and Leroy Scott and Gurley Flynn and Mabel Dodge and Margaret Sanger and Mary Craig Sinclair!

Also, meet that great statesman of letters, that strong Silent Man who has made more speeches than any other occupant of the White House, outdoing Carlyle with his gospel of silence in forty volumes. When civilization was in peril, Cautious Cal did not hesitate, but rushed to the rescue with a series of articles, " Enemies of the Republic," published in the *Delineator*, one of the Butterick chain, certified circulation 2,102,223 women per month; also an article in *Good Housekeeping*, one of the Hearst chain, certified circulation 1,150,947 women per month. Cal realized the importance of reaching the women because they were the ones who were destined to be nationalized by the Bolsheviks; also it pays to carry on propaganda among women, because they don't know any better than to believe what you tell them.

Also that other great artist, General Charles G. Dawes, violin-virtuoso and composer of a melody. Fritz Kreisler edited it—but of course not because the author is a millionaire banker, powerful enough to rob his stockholders of a couple of hundred thousand dollars to subsidize the master-corruptionist Lorimer. Recently Hell-and-Maria made a campaign tour of the country, and his progress was a tornado of " Melody by General Charles G. Dawes." Of course the reason why every radio station in his path played it several times every day was not that he was presiding officer of the Senate, which controls appointments to the new radio board, having power to seize all radio stations whenever Calvin or Charlie wish to call their political opponents Bolsheviks, as during the La Follette campaign. Keep your eye on Hell-and-Maria, for when American Fascism begins its march on Washington this great artist will be the Mussolini.

[59]

CHAPTER XIV

THE FASCIST CAREER

THERE are a number of great men in America whose
careers have been made wholly out of this militant
Mammonism. I am going to introduce you to one of
them, the Honourable Richard Washburn Child. Before
the war he was a minor novelist and Wall Street lawyer;
he became assistant to Frank Vanderlip in war finance
work and then, in face of the Bolshevik peril, he took
charge of *Collier's Weekly*, with its campaign for the
deportation of the reds. The question arose, who was to
be the next president of the United States, to carry out
this national house-cleaning.

After the lapse of seven years we can say—with the
backing of a unanimous decision of the United States
Supreme Court—that the nomination of Harding was a
conspiracy to loot the oil reserves of the United States
navy, as carefully planned and as definitely criminal as
any pirate raid. Harding was the chief of the " Ohio
gang," and he was put in to let that gang loot the nation,
as previously he had let it loot Ohio. The oil men put
up the money to carry the Republican convention, upon
the understanding that they would get the cabinet positions
necessary for the stealing of the naval reserves. To elect
their chosen one, the plutocracy contributed the biggest
campaign fund ever known in our history; and this money
was spent according to the new arts of propaganda learned
in the war days. You remember the Vigilantes and their

patriotic fervour? Well, here was another time to rally the writers and artists, the furnishers of ideas and inspirations, to persuade the American voters to turn over their government to a pirate band.

So, on a Saturday afternoon, the 25th of April, 1920, behold a special train of five parlour cars proceeding to Atlantic City, loaded with George Ade, Rex Beach, Porter Emerson Browne, Edna Ferber, Jesse L. Lasky, Mary Roberts Rinehart, Booth Tarkington, Charles Hanson Towne, William Allen White—if that train had run off the track, American culture would never have recovered! They had a banquet at the most expensive of hotels, and next morning the *New York Times* reported as follows:

" The mystery surrounding the identity of the backers of the week-end party of authors, movie managers, magazine writers, publicity agents, cartoonists and artists who arrived here to-night to hear prominent Republicans discourse on the ideals and policies of their party was partly dispelled when it was explained that the expenses of the junket were paid by Richard Washburn Child, one of its originators, with a special Republican subscription from the Republican National Committee."

Now, would the big chief of the Ohio gang fail to be grateful for a service of such distinction? The big chief would no more overlook it than he would fail to name the right cabinet members, so that the oil men might have their loot. Do not be surprised, therefore, to find that a couple of months after the inauguration, Mr. Richard Washburn Child is named Ambassador Extraordinary and Plenipotentiary to Italy.

He goes; and there falls to him the most thrilling adventure ever dreamed by a literary red-hunter. While he is in Rome—knee breeches, court receptions, and all the glories—the Italian workers rise and take possession of the factories in Russian style. But they have walked into a trap, because Italy has no coal, and the British fleet controls the sea, and the American bankers control all the credit in the world, and the would-be Bolsheviks of Italy cannot

[61]

turn a wheel.   While they are debating, in some confusion, what to do next, a renegade Italian Socialist comes to Mr. Child; they are the ones to hire, you understand, because they know the movement they are going to wreck, and have a special bitterness against it—look at my ex-Comrade Joe Patterson!

Mussolini's proposition is the simplest possible.   He will raise a slogan, and gather a band of young assassins, and seize Italy for the bankers; only he must have money for the job, and will the Americans give him a loan?   The Americans are just then in the business of subsidizing assassins all over the world—Kolchak, Denikin, Judenitch, Wrangel, Semenoff, Petlura, Horthy, Pilsudski, Manner-heim, I can't remember all the names.   It takes but a few minutes to settle such a question in these days of cables and high-powered executives.   Mussolini gets his loans, and more loans—during the year just past he got two hundred millions from Wall Street, and when his assassins are scattered by the outraged Italian workers, the American investing public will be left holding the sack—just as the French people were left after their bankers had led them to arm the Russian Tsar so that the French bankers might grab the iron of Lorraine; just as our American government is left after the House of Morgan led us into helping the French bankers out of their mess.

My morning mail comes, and here is a copy of the *Labour Defender*, with two photographs: " Italian Worker, Angelo Capanelli, before and after being blinded by Fascists." It is still going on, you see, the work for which the Wall Street bankers have paid your money.   I quote from the same paper : " Hundreds assassinated, thousands wounded, tens of thousands arrested and thousands of these sentenced to long prison terms.   The dimensions of the terror are almost incredible—Mussolini's regime puts the Neros and Borgias in the shade.   Murders, arrests, tortures, long imprisonment, searches, destroying and burning of homes and buildings; depriving the opposition of their freedom of speech and movement; banishment and deportation to sparsely inhabited Mediterranean islands——"

Flushed with rapture over such spectacles, the Honourable Richard Washburn Child comes home with the new gospel for America, and is made Fascist-in-Chief to the great central power-plant of reaction, the Curtis publications. He becomes, as you might say, their secretary of foreign relations, ambassador extraordinary and plenipotentiary to the capitalist world; keeping in touch with the wholesale assassins of Italy, Roumania, Hungary, Bulgaria, Poland, Finland and the Baltic provinces, China, Japan, India and Java, Mexico, Central and South America and the West Indies; surveying the job of slaughtering rebel workers, and portraying it to the American people as the saving of civilization and making the world safe for democracy.

And just a word more concerning those " authors, movie managers, magazine writers, publicity agents, cartoonists and arists," whom we left disporting themselves in Atlantic City at the expense of the Republican National Committee. Five years later the looting of America by the Republican party bandits had become such a horror that Mr. Child's old chief, Frank Vanderlip, was shocked into protest. He remembered the Vigilantes, with their slogans of patriotism and public service, and thought he would rally them for the grand patriotic work of kicking out the looters of our heritage. The treasurer of the organization called them to a dinner at the University Club in New York; but alas, they couldn't agree what to do—and so they did nothing! Would I be too cynical if I suggested that a few of them may have wondered who was going to pay the bills this time? And especially if the paymasters were prepared to give a life contract? It is a serious matter to ask a Vigilante to attack the interests which control every newspaper, magazine, and moving-picture company in the country where he has to earn his living!

CHAPTER XV

THE GREAT DOG LORRIMOR

Now let us survey what I have called the great central power-plant of Fascism in America, the Curtis publications, presided over by Colonel George Horace Lorimer. Another military title, you perceive—it was the governor of Kentucky who recognized the services of this great literary Fascist, and appointed him honorary colonel. Lorimer's training for the task of militarizing American culture was gained as secretary to Old Armour, the Chicago pork-butcher—one of whose intimates remarked to me, out of inside knowledge, " You're lucky that Old P.D. was not alive, or you'd never have lived to publish ' The Jungle.' " Colonel Lorimer put the wisdom of the stock-yards into one of the most cynical books ever written in America, " The Letters of a Self-Made Merchant to His Son." It is supposed to be funny, and it is, unless you happen to belong to one of four classes of beings —first, a hog, second, a stockyards worker, third, a consumer of meat, and fourth, a human being with heart or conscience.

Young Ogden Armour didn't have me killed; he tried for three days and nights to persuade his lawyers to let him have me arrested for criminal libel, and failing in that, he got Lorimer to have one of his hacks write a defence of the stockyards industry, which solemnly denied every one of the jokes which Lorimer had written about Ogden's father. And this is only one illustration of the service the *Saturday Evening Post* has performed for predatory wealth, during the fifteen hundred weeks that I have been watching it. They are so big and so powerful that the truth matters to them no more than a flea-bite. I showed in " The Brass Check " how they deliberately distorted the facts and then refused correction; and their answer to " The Brass Check " was to add another million to their weekly circulation.

From the point of view of the literary business man, these Curtis publications are perfection. They read your manuscripts promptly, and pay the very highest price upon acceptance. So they are the goal of every young writer's ambition, and the most corrupting force in American letters. Their stuff is as standardized as soda crackers; originality is taboo, new ideas are treason, social sympathy is a crime, and the one virtue of man is to produce larger and larger quantities of material things. They have raised up a school of writers, panoplied in prejudice, a lynching squad to deal with every sign of protest against the ideals of plutocracy.

Take Emerson Hough—Major Hough, I believe it is proper to call him. Once he was an amiable teller of outdoor tales and frontier histories, and in " John Rawn " he even showed traces of social understanding. But the war turned him into an Iroquois Indian. He joined the Intelligence Service, and when the White Terror began he joined Colonel Lorimer. I don't think I have ever read in an American magazine any writing more vicious than the articles he contributed to the *Saturday Evening Post*, glorying in the raids upon the " reds "; " The Round-up," I remember, was the title of one, but no ranchman ever hated his cattle, nor caused them needless suffering. When police detectives stamped their heels into the faces of Russian-Jewish working-girls, Major Hough literally screamed with glee. He died two or three years later, and no doubt the celestial authorities are providing him an unlimited supply of Russian-Jewish working-girls to be stamped upon.

[65]   E

Or my old friend Isaac Marcosson. You may read in Ike's book, " Adventures in Interviewing," how, as publicity agent for Doubleday-Page, he made the fame of " The Jungle "—you will almost think he wrote it. But don't get the idea that there was anything " pink " about Ike; no, he is a publicity man according to the Lorimer standard, he promotes whatever his boss has to sell. Of late years, having Lorimer as boss, Ike has promoted the wholesale murder of those same poor devils whom in the " Jungle " days he professionally pitied. He has become a kind of travelling sales agent for reaction; he has done Soviet Russia, Central Europe and the Orient, and just recently Mexico; and always he comes home with a series of articles for his boss, proving the standardized doctrine that the masters of world capitalism are benevolent supermen engaged in conferring the blessings of civilization upon the inferior races, but having their efforts imperilled by evil-minded intriguers called " reds."

Twenty years ago there were appearing in *McClure's Magazine*—then a free paper with a real editor—a number of extraordinary short stories. There was a series dealing with Wall Street, and I remember the " white bondworm " who spent his time in the great underground vaults; also a series called " Butterflies," dealing with the pitiful chorus girls and artist models, and their efforts, not often successful, to fight off the predatory males who control the purse-strings in the art business. These stories were real literature, full of pity and insight and penetrating social criticism. With my usual custom of butting in on things, I tried hard to find some publisher to bring them out in book-form. I failed; and I suppose that George Kibbe Turner was starved out—anyhow, he went into the Lorimer kennel, and at the height of the reaction wrote a silly and stupid anti-radical yarn, " Red Friday "; also some short stories—I described one of them in " The Brass Check " : " a short story, which turns out not to be a short story at all, but a piece of preaching upon the following grave and weighty theme; that the trouble with America is that everybody is spending too much money; that the railroad brotherhoods are proposing to turn robbers and take away the property of their masters; and that a working-man who is so foolish as to buy a piano for his daughter will discover that he has ruined himself to no purpose, because working-men's daughters ought not to have pianos —they are too tired to play them when they get through with their work! "

And Harry Leon Wilson. Here was man with all the makings of a novelist. Twenty-five years ago he wrote " The Spenders," a book that dealt with reality; but now his charm and humour are wasted upon the empty sugar-and-water themes required by Lorimer. At the height of the White Terror he made his contribution to the task of keeping America capitalist—a tale about some workers who took over a factory and tried to run it, and the absurd mess they made. So it was taught to *Saturday Evening Post* readers ten years ago; and not even yet has Lorimer let them learn that the Soviets have got production back to the pre-war standard.

Or my friend Nina Wilcox Putnam. Would you ever dream, to read the rubbish that she ladles into the Lorimer soup-kettle, that she possesses real brains, and wit, and radical sympathy? That is when you listen to her talk. But alas, we " reds " have no paymasters, and Nina has no social conscience. I could tell you about others—but it makes me sad, and, I conclude with my friend Sinclair Lewis, who lived in the kennel for many years, but jumped over the fence. He told me how Lorimer took " Main Street " as a personal affront, and vowed to " get " its author. Also George Sterling—who summed up his country in four special antipathies—" jazz, free verse, the movies, and the *Saturday Evening Post*." Some years ago he contributed to the *Masses* a wild and terrible poem, and I reproduce it here without giving you any hint what it all means.

THE BLACK HOUND BAYS

If the young folk build an altar to the beautiful and true,
Be sure the great dog Lorrimor shall lift a leg thereto.

The lords of the nation go hunting with their dogs;
Some have the heart of tigers and some the heart of hogs.
On the path of the quarry the yapping mongrels pour,
And the keenest of the pack is the great dog Lorrimor.

" Woo-hoo-hoo-hoo!   O lords, spare not the spur!
Give me the white doe, Freedom, that I flesh my fangs in her!
I ha' hate for all wild hearts! " bays the dog Lorrimor.

The men of the law make up the sniffing pack;
The writers of tales go forth upon the track;
The vendors of the news are zealous in the fore,
And loudest of the chase is the great dog Lorrimor.

" Give me the young, lest the lips of youth blaspheme!
Give me the rebel and the dreamer of the dream!
Give me your foe, that you see his entrails steam! "

Oh, lavish is his tongue for the feet of all his lords!
And hoarse is his throat if a foot go near their hoards.
Sharp are his teeth and savage is his heart,
When he lifts up his voice to drown the song of Art.

" Master, be kind, for I, I too am rich!
I ha' buried many bones, tho' my ageing hide do itch.
I ha' buried many bones where the snowy lilies were.
I ha' made that garden mine," bays the dog Lorrimor.

He crouches at their feet and is glad of his collar
And the brand on his rump of the consecrated dollar.
For the humble at the gate he is loud in his wrath;
But no sound shall be heard when the strong are on the Path.

" Give me the minstrel, the faun and wanderer;
Give me high Beauty—she shall know me for your cur!
Woo-hoo-hoo-hoo! " bays the dog Lorrimor.

If the young folk build an altar to their vision of the New,
Be sure the great dog Lorrimor shall lift a leg thereto.

CHAPTER XVI

ART AND THE TRADER

Every artist is a double personality, living two lives. The impulse of art is a spiritual overflow; the artist absorbs life, works it over, recreates it, and pours it out, to enrich and fructify the lives of others. The impulse is in its very essence altruistic, bountiful as Nature, unselfish as God. But also, alas, the artist is a creature with a stomach that must be filled and a skin that must be covered; he is apt to want a wife, or a husband, and children, and these also must be fed and covered, and the wife must have a social position among the other wives. So the godlike impulse of spiritual overflow is checked and censored; there are copyrights and contracts and royalties and foreign and dramatic and second serial rights.

This dual nature is shared by every form of art product. A book is what Milton calls it, the precious life-blood of a master-spirit, embalmed and treasured up on purpose to a life beyond life. To be sure; but also a book is a piece of merchandise, upon which toll must be paid to lumbermen and paper-mills and railroads and printers and publishers and jobbers and retailers. So it comes that at every minute of his life the artist is at war with himself. " I feel two natures struggling within me," says the sculptor Barnard; and maybe he doesn't know how this happens, but I can tell him, having supported myself by my art for thirty-three years, and been practically never out of debt in one form or another. As publisher of my own books, I face the conflict every time I have a new one ready. Shall

I put the price lower, and reach some thousands of additional readers? Or shall I put it higher, and reduce my unfavourable balance at the printers?

It was my fortune many years ago to sit in the sumptuous work-rooms of Mr. David Belasco, while Arch Selwyn, then a play-broker, was engaged in selling the script of my play, " The Millennium." Both these gentlemen belong to a race which has been in trade for many thousands of years; you may watch their technique along the kerb where the suspender-merchants assemble. In this case the object of the barter is a work of art; and, strange as it may seem, both traders have a keen appreciation of art qualities. " Yes, delightful, I know," says Mr. Belasco, " but oh, my God, think what it's going to cost to produce —and all that Socialist stuff in it—I'll be bankrupt if I have to pay more than two hundred and fifty advance." I sit and listen—it is my chance to write other plays that is being decided.

Also I have been present while Charlie Chaplin was selling the fruit of his genius to the traders; at least, I haven't actually been there, but Charlie has enacted the scene for me, and that is the same thing. He is under contract to make a two-reel picture, and out of his spiritual overflow he has made eight or ten—it is " The Kid." And the traders come, great hulks of flesh rolling out of their limousines, and they sit slouched in their chairs, and the reels are unrolled before them, and the sensitive artist sits quivering—he can't keep still while his reels are being unrolled, his hands become frantic, he must hear you speak. " What do you think of it? Is it good? " But the traders do not speak, they understand how to wring the artist soul. How Charlie loathes them—his form swells to greater bulk as he enacts them, his face becomes a grim mask; there comes a grunt, from under the chest, and one great hog looks at the next great hog, and at last a verdict: " Vun million is enough, huh? " And the other grunts, " Vun is too much."

Such is the life of artists under capitalism. And do not

think that I am lacking in pity for any artist—my harshest words are merely an effort to goad him into class consciousness. For it is not merely his individual life that is at stake, not merely his art, but civilization. " If the salt have lost its savour, wherewith shall it be salted? "

The successful artists are those who learn to put a shell around them, and live like a tortoise, inside. The trouble with this procedure is that in the course of time the creature is apt to become all shell and no tortoise; the art impulses die, and only imitation and pose are left. I remember once at Helicon Hall we had a visit from a newspaper poet—I have forgotten his name, and wouldn't give it anyhow, because he was a poor devil, and I am after the rich ones. He sat in front of our fire-place for a couple of hours and talked about his art, and it turned out to be the art of marketing verses, and the personalities of the various editors, and what they paid, and what kind of " stuff " they preferred. " I sold him a poem once, but they don't buy much from outsiders," and so on and on.

At that same conference sat two ladies, whom I knew well. They were taking care of themselves and a couple of children by their pens, and it was a perfectly cold-blooded business proposition, and no nonsense. In some months of acquaintance, I do not think I ever heard either of these ladies express an opinion of a book unless it had to do with what the author had got for it, and for other books, and how that magazine or publisher compared with others. I had contempt for such an attitude; until it happened that the younger of the ladies, a jolly soul, recited quite casually how she had sought a position on the greatest of New York newspapers, and had been pulled down on to the lap of the wealthy and famous publisher. So then I realized a new point of view : the fact that this young woman could turn out a regular, standard product, good for two or three thousand dollars a year, meant the ability to slap the face of the great newspaper proprietor and walk out of his office. Twenty years ago a leading actress on Broadway remarked to me, " I know practically all the successful women of the stage, and I know only one who did not sell herself to get her start." And it happened that quite recently the very same remark was made to me by one of the leading film stars of Hollywood. No, you can't blame the women for becoming commercial!

I was for a while a member of the executive body of the Author's League of America, and we met for luncheon now and then to decide the fate of American letters. A fellow-member was Rex Beach, and I happened to ask him, " Why did you start to write? " The answer came in a flash, " Because I found I could make more money than by mining gold." We may say that this proves Mr. Beach an honest man; but also it proves him not an artist. If he had been the latter, he would have replied, just as promptly, and just as honestly, " Because I have something to say, and all the money in New York couldn't hire me to do anything else." And it is a fact that when business men, however honest, are permitted to crowd the real artist out of existence, culture dies. It is necessary to exclude business men from the writing field, and also from the selecting of writers, and the control of the channels between writers and public.

What, exactly, is the difference between literature and journalism. The maker of literature strives to say a thing once and for all time; while the journalist says it over and over, with slight variations, every day or week or month. And since ninety-nine per cent. of the money paid out for written words is paid for journalism, it follows that ninety-nine per cent. of the writers must be journalists, no matter what capacity they may have to produce literature. I charge the big commercial magazines with applying to the written word the American methods of standardization and mass production, and you think perhaps that I am playful; but that is only because you don't face the facts. A modern editor is the head of a department in a huge manufacturing plant; he has to have so-and-so much copy at regular intervals, to fill up the spaces between advertisements of soaps and cigarettes and automobiles; so much bait to lure the public into his advertisement-trap. And when he finds that a certain kind of bait does the business, he orders more of that kind, and offers a price so high that no author's wife can resist it.

Once upon a time Finlay Peter Dunne wrote a sketch about a shrewd and witty Irishman; and what happened? Why, simply that Mr. Dunne was commanded to write fifteen hundred such sketches—" Mr. Dooley " every Sunday for thirty years. In the same way Montague Glass has been commanded to write fifteen thousand paragraphs, in every one of which Potash or Perlmutter says " Gott sei Dank," or " Gott soll huten." In the same way Milt Gross has been commanded to be a " Nize Baby " for the next forty years. In the same way Jack London was commanded to repeat a hundred times his brief journey over the Alaskan snows, and Conan Doyle was compelled to bring Sherlock Holmes back to life after having mercifully killed him. And if you ask the question, would any of these writers have produced great literature anyhow, the answer is that every living thing does better in a good environment than in a bad one. If you let a garden run wild, you will have ill-smelling weeds; while if you tend it with love plus intelligence, you may have flowers of greater beauty than the most optimistic seed-catalogue has predicted.

CHAPTER XVII

INCENSE TO MAMMON

RULING classes have existed for a long time in the world, and have built themselves a mighty structure of prestige. Reverence for the great and noble ones of the earth is implicit in all the fairy-tales of childhood, and sanctified by a monarchist and autocratic religion. Literature and art are full of it—I have never made a count, but I would wager that nine-tenths of the heroes and heroines of all fiction and drama are persons of social importance: the classics without any exception, Greek, Roman and French; Shakespeare, and everything in English literature, excepting the comic parts, down to quite recent times. It would be interesting to take a list of the best sellers for the past twenty years, British and American, and study the social status of the heroes and heroines. In the British case, you would find the noble titles exceeding by ten thousand per cent. the actual proportion of such titles to the living population; in the case of America you would find that fifty per cent. of all heroes are wealthy at the outset, and another forty-nine per cent. become so before the end of the story. You might safely offer a prize of ten thousand dollars for the discovery of a best-selling hero who was wealthy at the beginning of the story and poor at the end.

The average author is, fundamentally, a naïve and trusting creature—half a child, or the make-believe impulse would not survive in him. Like all children, he believes what the grown-ups tell him, and is impressed by the princes of real life, just as by those in the fairy-tales. So in this opulent capitalist era, a great many writers do not have to be purchased, but serve privilege gladly and with spontaneous awe. Chief among them is a celebrated lady whose work I have been watching for twenty-three years, carrying on with her all that time a sort of literary lover's quarrel—off again, on again, gone again, as Finegan puts it. Just now we are " on," but I can't be sure what will happen when this chapter sees the light.

In the year 1904 Gertrude Atherton (she forbids me to call her " Mrs. Atherton ") published in the *Atlantic Monthly* an article asking why American literature was so bourgeois. She was using the word in the old French sense of " middle-class," rather than the modern Russian sense of " capitalist." She found our literature tame and conventional and dull, whereas she thought it ought to be big and bold and noisy. I wrote an answer, which the great *Atlantic* rejected, but which *Collier's* published. I said :

" The bourgeoisie is that class which, all over the world, takes the sceptre of power as it falls from the hands of the aristocracy; which has the skill and cunning to survive in the free-for-all combat which follows upon the political revolution. Its dominion is based upon wealth; and hence the determining characteristic of the bourgeois society is its regard for wealth. To it, wealth is power, it is the end and goal of things. The aristocrat knew nothing of the possibility of revolution, and so he was bold and gay. The bourgeois does know about the possibility of revolution, and so it is that Gertrude Atherton finds that American literature is ' timid.' She finds it ' anæmic,' simply because the bourgeois ideal knows nothing of the spirit, and tolerates intellectual activity only for the ends of commerce and material welfare. She finds also that it ' bows before the fetish of the body,' and she is much perplexed by the discovery. She does not seem to understand that the bourgeois represents an achievement of the body, and that all he knows in the world is body. He is well fed himself, his wife is stout, and his children are

[75]

fine and vigorous.   He lives in a big house, and wears the latest thing in clothes; his civilization furnishes these to everyone—at least to everyone who amounts to anything; and beyond that the bourgeois understands nothing—save only the desire to be entertained. . . .

" So we come to literature—and to the author.   The bourgeois recognizes the novelist and the poet as a means of amusement somewhat above the prostitute, and about on a level with the music-hall artist; he recognizes the essayist, the historian and the publicist as agents of bourgeois repression equally as necessary as the clergyman and the editor.   To all of them he grants the good things of the bourgeois life, a bourgeois home with servants who know their places, and a bourgeois club with smiling and obsequious waiters.   They may even, on state occasions, become acquainted with the bourgeois magnates, and touch the gracious fingers of the magnates' pudgy wives.   There is only one condition, so obvious that it hardly needs to be mentioned—they must be bourgeois, they must see life from the bourgeois point of view.   Beyond that there is not the least restriction; the novelist, for instance, may roam the whole of space and time—there is nothing in life that he may not treat, provided only that he be bourgeois in his treatment.   He may show us the olden time, with noble dames and gallant gentlemen dallying with graceful sentiment.   He may entertain us with pictures of the modern world, may dazzle us with visions of high society in all its splendours, may awe us with the wonders of modern civilization, of steam and electricity, the flying-machine and the automobile.   He may thrill us with battle, murder and Sherlock Holmes.   He may bring tears to our eyes at the thought of the old folks at home, or at his pictures of the honesty, humility and sobriety of the common man; he may even go to the slums and show us the ways of Mrs. Wiggs, her patient frugality and beautiful contentment in that state of life to which it has pleased God to call her.   In any of these fields the author, if he is worth his salt, may be ' entertaining '—and so the royalties will come in. If there is anyone whom this does not suit—who is so perverse that the bourgeois do not please him, or so obstinate that he will not learn to please the bourgeois—we send after him our literary police-man, the bourgeois reviewer, and bludgeon him into silence; or better yet, we simply leave him alone, and he moves into a garret. . . .

" These are the conditions under which our literature is produced, and which account for all the qualities in it which Gertrude Atherton has perceived but cannot explain. A better witness than Gertrude Atherton could not be had, for she herself is one of the most bourgeois of our writers. We have no writer more readily impressed with bigness than Gertrude Atherton, more ready to accept it as great-ness. It was the opinion of Shelley that ' poets are the acknowledged legislators of mankind '; in Gertrude Atherton's opinion the ' Rulers of Kings ' are not poets, nor are they prophets and saints, with their visions and aspirations; they are simply the extra-heavy bourgeoisie. Gertrude Atherton measures the greatness of a man by the standard of the Indian chief—by the number of squaws he has; she knows nothing of the facts of life which make it true that one woman can be more to a man than ten women can possibly be—which simply means that she is not acquainted with the phenomenon of spirituality."

Thirteen years passed, and Gertrude Atherton, horror-stricken by the war, published a novel called " The White Morning," dealing with an imaginary revolution in Germany. I had my own magazine then, and reviewed the book, pointing out an interesting sign of the times: for the first time in her life this novelist was willing to approve a revolt against an aristocracy. But her prophecy was unscientific. " The heroine is a rich German lady, and she kills rich German men, which is in violation of an elementary principle of revolutionary economics. With-out meaning to be dogmatic, I will venture to say to Gertrude Atherton : " When the revolt in Germany comes —and it is very nearly due—you will not see rich German

women killing rich German men; you will see rich
German women killing poor German women, and calling
on rich German men to help." That prophecy was made
in June, 1918; and the Spartacist revolt came a year later.

I welcomed Gertrude Atherton as a new recruit to the
ranks of social reconstructors. But alas, President Wilson
began his private war on the Russian revolution, and I
began my war on him, and Gertrude Atherton flew into
a towering rage with me, and wrote me that I was " no
better than a Bolshevik," and she would have nothing
more to do with me. She even wrote an article for that
most odious of publications, the *National Civic Federation
Review*, attacking me for having used her favourable
opinion of " Jimmie Higgins," after I knew that she dis-
approved the ending of the book. That had happened
by accident—the opinion had already been published, and
was reprinted as a matter of office routine; really, I thought
I ought to have had a request to cease using it, instead of
a slashing in Ralph Easley's snarl-paper.

More years passed, and I ran into Gertrude Atherton at
a dinner of the P.E.N. Club in San Francisco. It was
just after the publication of " Black Oxen," and I asked
the author of this " rejuvenation " novel some personal
questions about the cause of her youthful appearance, and
she replied that it was none of my damn business; which
caused great hilarity among the assembled gentlemen and
lady authors. But my enemy came to hear me lecture on
" Mammonart," and said so many nice things that I
couldn't quote them, and invited me to tea at the
St. Francis. I had an idea that if that tea-party could
have lasted a month, instead of an hour, I could have told
Gertrude Atherton so much about her heroes, the " Rulers
of Kings," and the mess they are making of their world,
as to shake just a little her lifelong trust in them. She is
honest, and has a conscience; it is the facts that are lacking
in her equipment.

After thirty-five years of offering incense to Mammon,
Gertrude Atherton has apparently not found spiritual peace

with her deity. " Black Oxen " comes as a kind of life-confession; the novelist puts herself into the soul of an elderly woman, rejuvenated by a miracle of science, and comes back from Europe to inspect New York society. A more devastating picture of waste, futility, and above all, boredom, could not be drawn by a muckraker's pen. It is difficult, in dealing with " realistic " fiction, to be sure just how much of this impression is intended. What, for instance, does Gertrude Atherton think of the libations of liquor which are poured out before the throne of Mammon in his metropolis? There is hardly a chapter of her book in which somebody doesn't take a drink of something alcoholic, and all the great ceremonials and crises of the story are preceded by and accompanied by a number of rounds of all varieties of booze. The old people drink, and the young people drink, and likewise they all hate one another—except when they are making love; and some-times they do both at the same time.

To me, of course, the most interesting part of the novel is its commentary on political and social theories. Quite casually, in passing from tea-party to dinner-table, and from dinner-table to grand opera, Gertrude Atherton solves the problems of our distracted age. For example, the problem of war, and the peace settlement which is worse than war. The novelist admits that our statesmen are blunderers and nincompoops, but she explains that our disillusionment, after the glorious thrills of wartime, is a mistake; we must go on having wars, and wait for evolu-tion to bring us to a state of development where we will stop having wars. Those foolish people who have the idea of stopping wars now, without waiting for evolution, will feel themselves properly rebuked by Gertrude Atherton, and will subside into their places; and likewise all revolutionists and Socialist agitators, whom the novelist completely annihilates with her sarcasms. She makes clear how dangerous it is to let the ignorant mob, which can understand nothing except revenge, have anything to do with trying to remedy social injustice. We must wait

a thousand years, until our ruling classes have acquired
sufficient intelligence to do things better; and if we want
to see how they are learning to do things better, all we
have to do is to read " Black Oxen," and watch them
gambling and drinking and idling and dressing up, and
going from tea-parties to dinners, and from dinners to
grand operas, murdering one another's reputations, seduc-
ing one another's wives, and always and everywhere being
what they consider brilliant and fascinating and wonderful
and prominent and famous and great.

CHAPTER XVIII

ROMANCE AND REACTION

In the days of my youth, one of the triumphs of the literary season was a " romantic " novel, " Monsieur Beaucaire," written by a young graduate of Princeton. The word " romantic," as a book-trade term, means the fragrance of vanished elegance; and this young author, who had been born on the banks of the Wabash, had yearned himself away to the far-off, departed glories of fashionable society in Bath.   How we did thrill with rage over the social snubs administered to the adventurous French barber; and how we shivered with ecstasy when it turned out that our dashing hero was no less a personage than His Highness Prince Louis-Philippe de Valois, Duke of Orleans, Duke of Chartres, Duke of Nemours, Duke of Montpensier, First Prince of the blood royal, First Peer of France, Lieutenant-General of French Infantry, Governor of Dauphiné, Knight of the Golden Fleece, Grand Master of the Order of Notre Dame, of Mt. Carmel and of St. Lazarus in Jerusalem, and cousin to his most Christian Majesty, Louis the Fifteenth, King of France.   It was a liberal education simply to repeat such a list of titles.

So I learned to know Booth Tarkington, and for a generation have watched him interpret the well-to-do classes of the Middle West, and make them gracious and charming for Colonel Lorimer.   Once Mr. Tarkington fooled me—I thought he was on the way to growing up. He wrote a novel called " The Turmoil," telling some truth about our industrial squalor; but, alas, the rebellious young hero performed the established fictional duty of marrying a pure girl of the leisure class, and living happy ever after upon the income of his father's greed.

And now Mr. Tarkington has apparently decided to enroll himself among the " diehard " Tories. The girding of the " reds " at his prosperous and agreeable capitalist world has driven him into a sort of " To hell with you " mood. You remember, back in the old muck-raking days, a cartoonist by the name of Opper, with his stock figure of " the trusts," fat and gross and wearing a checked suit with a dollar mark in every check? Well, Mr. Tarkington has taken this figure for the hero of a novel called " The Plutocrat "; putting him on a palatial steamship and sending him over to Europe to do all those things which have made our name a by-word—bellowing and bragging, scattering his dollars about and jeering at the relics of ancient culture. The advertising men, needless to say, were enraptured with such a hero, and prepared for this best-seller a series of cartoons representing a " rah-rah boy " parading down the street, ringing a bell with one hand and waving an American flag with the other, shouting defiance to all enemies of Mammon. Needless to say, it is from the palatial establishment of Doubleday, Page & Company that this patriotic demonstration emanates.

As foil to his hero-plutocrat Mr. Tarkington provides a feeble-souled creature, alleged to be a New York editor; his collapse at the end serves as a warning to all young men who may be tempted to think or speak irreverently of a plutocrat. This editor is an " intellectual," and hundred per cent. literature makes plain that such persons have become a source of intense annoyance to our propertied classes. Colonel Lorimer can hardly get out an issue of his paper without a sneer at them. On the whole I should say that the editors of the *New Republic* have cause to be well pleased with their achievements to date.

And Major Rupert Hughes—another military title. He has been a gracious host to me, and I am pained to have to point out the economic implications of his writings. Major Hughes also goes in for " romance," the aristocratic elegance of our ancestors. If he strives to prove that the morals of these ancestors were the same as those of Hollywood, you are not to assume that he means impoliteness to our ancestors. " The Golden Ladder " is a lively tale about an adventurous lady who rose from the gutter to vast wealth, and intimacy with Gertrude Atherton's royal-souled hero, the " Conqueror," Alexander Hamilton. And then " Souls for Sale," very shrewdly disguised propaganda for the glories of high-salaried Hollywood; it made a marvellously successful picture, and in the middle of it you saw the film queens parading, one after another in their own persons, each one duly labelled. Never was there such a box-office rush!

Nor must this discussion of romance omit Elinor Glyn, who has succeeded Ouida as high priestess of luxurious love. Like Ouida, she adds a touch of preachment as a sop to the censor. These preachments take place upon tiger-skin rugs and silken couches; and when they are made into pictures, Madame Glyn personally supervises the local colour. I had the honour of sitting next to her at a dinner-party in Hollywood, and she explained to me gravely the high philosophical aims of her sex writings. I was duly impressed; but for some reason, when I went home and told my wife about it, I was not able to communicate the impression. I cannot understand why the ladies are so sceptical of one another; so it will be better if I confine my discussion to our male romancers.

For example, Wallace Irwin; an old-time newspaper man from San Francisco, who came to New York and was introduced to high society by Robbie Collier. In those old days he wrote about a Japanese schoolboy, who was jolly fun; also he was permitted by young Robbie to write vigorous satiric verse exposing the brutality of big

business.   But now, alas, Robbie is dead, and the art of
satire has died with him; Colonel Lorimer has taken his
place as paymaster to Wallace Irwin, and the poet makes
pitiful efforts to be funny while kotowing before an
idol of Cal Coolidge.   Also he makes his bow as a serious
novelist—and of course the thing he is serious about is
the efforts of the fashionable rich to solve their sexual
problems.   " Lew Tyler's Wives "—you can see that
they have to make several tries; and " The Golden Bed "
—could anyone imagine a more fetching title for a best-
seller?   Could anyone imagine a heroine more romantic
than this delicate, soft, wayward, impulsive but lovable
rich Southern girl?   She is adored by a great plutocrat
of candy, but does not appreciate his rugged heart, and
so ends in tragedy; but do not let that worry you, it
is the conventional fate of beautiful queens, in modern
plutocracy as in ancient aristocracy.   " Why are they
called dynasties? " the professor of history once asked
me, and I answered, " Because that is what they always
seem to do."

And   then   Major   Stewart   Edward   White—another
military man, you note.   When I was young, Major
White made his great hit with " The Blazed Trail," and
I, in my capacity as Socialist agitator, wrote him a letter
asking if he had stopped to realize the social implications
of his story of the lumber-camps.   The workers had
exhausted themselves to make a great business coup for
the rich young owner—some had actually got themselves
killed in excess of loyalty; and at the end of the book
we leave them cheering themselves hoarse over the
marriage of the triumphant young owner to the lovely
rich heroine—and never one hint that there is anything
coming to the workers, that they have any claim to share
in the wealth they have created.

Major White took my criticism with courtesy.   " I
reported what I saw," he wrote me—the stock defence
of the novelist.   Is it true, or merely a way of fooling
yourself?   Time passed, and the truth which was so

apparent to me, began to reach the slower brains of the toilers in the lumber-camps; then Major White saw a new set of phenomena—these labourers stopped cheering for their rich young owner and his bride, and took to organizing and working out a social philosophy, and publishing papers and magazines, and preparing themselves to take over the social heritage out of which they had been cheated in " The Blazed Trail." We saw the owners bring in their spies and private detectives, their sheriffs and militia, and proceed to crush that worker's movement by a campaign of savagery combined with wholesale perjury. We saw the American Legion, of which Major White is a proud member, set out to mob a hall of the I.W.W. and lynch its inmates, and we saw the entire power of the press of America turned to lying about the incident, and the entire power of the capitalist courts set to jailing the victims for life.

Here was a full-sized theme for a great novelist; here was something Major White might have " seen," by the simple process of turning his eyes in that direction. Did he do so? He did not. Would I be too crude if I should point out that Colonel Lorimer would have turned down his thumbs on a story telling the truth about the Centralia massacre? The Major went off to hunt lions in Africa, and prove that they could be killed with a bow and arrow; an expensive and aristocratic thing to do, and a sure-fire hit with the Colonel. I grant you that to kill the lions of Africa with a bow and arrow is a man-sized job; but what about killing the lions of organized greed with a pen?

The task of portraying the " wobblies " was left to another " romantic " novelist, Zane Grey. Dr. Grey—who began his life at the more useful work of dentistry—wrote a novel " The Desert of Wheat," in which he portrayed the industrial workers as degenerates and criminals, whose occupations were burning barns and crops, and abducting beautiful heroines. It has been my fortune to meet some hundreds of " wobblies "—

 MONEY WRITES !

They have a way of coming to see me when they get out of jail, and telling me what has happened to them. They are men with souls of steel, tried in a fiery furnace. I happened to see the filming of the moving picture made from Dr. Grey's romance, and could discover no resemblance between the haggard martyr faces I knew, and the moron types selected by the casting director.

It happened that shortly afterwards I met Dr. Grey personally, at a ball in the home of a moving-picture producer. We were standing on the side-lines watching the show—since neither of us happens to be an ornamental or festive person. Desiring to be affable, I remarked, " I have noticed a curious thing—I make my heroes out of the same fellows that you make your villains of." I don't remember what Dr. Grey replied, but I learned afterwards that my remark had caused him great uneasiness. He repeated it to our host, asking plaintively, " How do you suppose anybody could make heroes out of my villains? "

And while we are listing the great romantic champions of hundred per cent. Americanism, let us not overlook Harold Bell Wright. Rev. Wright—he began as a Christian (Disciples) clergyman—has evolved out of his inner consciousness an America of the open spaces, vast, clean and wholesome, a Christian (Disciples) clergyman's wish-fulfilment. In this romantic America, virtue is always rewarded at page five hundred and something, with good common-sense rewards such as good common-sense Americans appreciate. As to the relationship which this romance bears to reality, the figures have been worked out by a mathematician—one of those bright young writers for the *New Republic* whom the hundred per centers so cordially despise. This young writer studied Rev. Wright's novel, " The Re-Creation of Brian Kent," according to the laws of compound mathematical probability, and I summarize briefly :

The hero, a criminal fleeing from justice in Chicago, arrives in a village in the Ozarks, the home of " Auntie

[86]

Sue, the silver-haired and golden-hearted re-creator."
Estimating that there are three thousand villages to which
he might have fled, we have an initial probability of one
in three thousand. The hero, drunk, drifts upon a
roaring river, and it would take a hydrographic chart to
determine the chances of his boat stopping on a certain
sand-bar; but we figure conservatively one chance in two
hundred, which makes the cumulative probability one
in six hundred thousand. Auntie Sue has sent some
Brazilian bank-notes to the Chicago bank which the hero
has robbed, and as there are eight thousand banks in
America, that is an item easy to figure. The notes
arrived on the very day that the hero could steal them,
which introduces yet another element of uncertainty.

It is a very long novel, and there enter such elements
as Auntie Sue's happening to select just the right one out
of thirty thousand stenographers in the United States,
to come and type the hero's manuscript; also the chance
of the hero's faithless wife with her paramour selecting
a cottage just across the river for a summer resort. With
such striking coincidences, the odds mount up fast, and
when we get to the end we find that the chances of this
particular wish-fulfilment of a Christian (Disciples) clergyman ever being brought about by a law-abiding Providence
are one in 3456 followed by thirty-two ciphers; or if you
find it easier to say, one chance in three hundred and
forty-five billion and six hundred millions of thousands
of millions of millions of billions.

CHAPTER XIX

THE IVORY TOWER

THE struggle of the disinherited of the earth against their oppressors has been going on for a long time; and history makes clear that it is no joke to be on the side of the oppressed. The masters will crucify you, as they did Jesus, or stab you to death as they did the Gracchi and Wat Tyler. If you are a great writer they will exile you with Dante and Hugo, or throw you into prison with Tasso and Dostoyevski and Ernst Toller and Ralph Chaplin. Since it is difficult to be sure which side is going to win, there is a tendency on the part of writers to say, " A plague on both your houses," and withdraw into an ivory tower of art.

And since, whatever men do, they have to make it seem noble and sublime, there arises a cult of haughty superiority to political problems; the artist becomes a semi-divine being, engaged in an activity of permanent significance, and the polishing of one of his phrases becomes more important than the fate of an empire. Such an artist will be an exponent of technique, a painter of the outsides of things; and necessarily, he will work to please the rich. Ivory towers cost money, and the artist must find patrons enough to pay the upkeep, and the wages of the cook and the gardener and the chamber-maid and the chauffeur and the doctor and the dentist and the bootlegger.

The tallest ivory tower in the United States is known as " Dower House," and is located near the town of

West Chester, Pennsylvania, an ultra-fashionable suburb
of the opulent city of Philadelphia. And if I take you
inside this " Dower House," and introduce you to the
master and mistress and the servants, and tell you what
they do and what they say and what they eat and what
they wear, do not suspect me of violating the laws of
hospitality, or of spying upon a fellow-craftsman : no,
the owner of the tower has invited the public inside, and
what I tell you is what Joseph Hergesheimer consents
for you to know. It is a book called " From an Old
House," advertised by the publishers as a work upon
American colonial furniture and landscape gardening, but
in reality the spiritual confession of an ivory tower artist.

My acquaintance with Mr. Hergesheimer is confined to
the exchange of a few sentences in an hotel lobby; just
enough to know what he looks like. It is not my fault
if I see his short and solid figure encased in brocaded
pyjamas of burnt orange and cerulean and glass green;
because he opened up one of his magazine articles with a
picture of himself making such a purchase in Chinatown
of San Francisco. Such things are part of your equipment, when you get your training in an art school, and
are obsessed by colour and form and the external details
of things, and devoting your life to fixing them in words,
to be printed on book paper and bound in expensive form
and sold to rich people, in order to teach them how to
spend their money upon colour and form and the external
details of things, in order that you, the ivory tower artist,
may have great sums to spend in the same way. And
do not think that I am being mean—I am merely
summarizing the artist's own statement of his interests
and activities.

How shall I convey to you a sense of the ineffable
exclusiveness of the fashionable society of West Chester?
The gentlemen dress themselves in pink hunting-coats
and the ladies in riding habits, and before dawn on
autumn mornings they ride out to chase foxes over the
country, to the music of horns and the bellowing of

hounds from the West Chester Hunt Kennels.   They
even have " gentlemen cricketers " in the neighbourhood.
And into this sacred circle comes an impecunious artist
trying to be a writer, and he marries a daughter of the
élite—her name is Dorothy, and her relatives are sniffy
at the wedding ceremony.   But he makes good, oh, most
gloriously; a sort of refined and highbrow Horatio Alger
story.

He buys an old Dutch farm-house, and camping out
uncomfortably in it, practises putting colour and form
and the external detail of things into beautiful words;
he watches the fashionable society of West Chester, and
puts their manners and morals into colonial and revolutionary costumes, and West Chester society is so fascinated
that it buys the books, and the impecunious artist who
once stood outside the building of a great magazine,
lacking the courage to go in, now has the editors coming
to visit him.   Yes, he lives only an hour's motor ride
from the estate of Colonel Lorimer—that was hardly
playing fair with the rest of the writers of America, to
go to the Colonel's own hunting-ground and marry a
daughter of one of the reigning families!   And to bribe
the Colonel with a precious piece of antique furniture, a
walnut sideboard—surely that is cheating at the game of
selling serials!

Anyhow, here is the money; and the proprietor of
" Dower House " tells with semi-playful charm how he
fell under the spell of ancient things, and how the
architects and builders and landscape gardeners conspired
with Dorothy to turn an old Pennsylvania Dutch farm-
house into " the estate of Joseph Hergesheimer "; how
they attended auctions, and bought this treasure and that,
and how the house was all built over, and decorated in
the fashion of our ancestors, and furnished with their
relics; so that now the artist can sit in any corner of any
room of his establishment, and see these ancient people
moving about their tasks, and make books out of their
imagined doings.   It is necessary that many books should

be written, because of the need of entertaining the pluto-cracy of Philadelphia in the fashion to which it is accustomed. You must not imagine that you can marry a daughter of West Chester good society for nothing! Nor imagine that any quantity of antiques will preserve your ivory tower from the inroads of change! Says Mr. Hergesheimer:

" In years gone by Dorothy had never perfumed her person with scented extracts, colognes; but now her dressing-table—the walnut lowboy carved with shells from Virginia—had its oddly shaped bottles with ornamental stoppers, its slender violet or green vials, from Paris; there was carmine lipstick, compact powder, in the various bags that everywhere accompanied her. This was a universal custom; I had arrived, after brief protests against a mere change, at the understanding that she couldn't, in her feminine sphere, be peculiar; but I wondered how, no longer than ten years ago, women had been so successfully seductive without such aids. Perhaps it was that the affair of seductiveness had, in itself, as an end, grown more important. I could see that the competition had become sharper, the rules were notably relaxed; lips to-day must be red, charm carried abroad on scent, at any price."

In this tallest of ivory towers in America our artist lives, surrounded by lowboys and highboys, field beds and hunting boards, Chippendale sofas and Windsor chairs, rat-tailed spoons and a Philadelphia silver tea-set. He tells us how he sits and gazes upon these objects, and dreams stories that are not stories, but merely characters to " hold together " the cupboards and pewter, the William and Mary chairs and Phyfe tables.

What stories come from such a source? " The Three Black Pennys "—a novel about three generations of Pennsylvania ironmasters, and how they loved ladies of that charm which ivory tower artists require in ladies, and how their line thinned out into elegant sterility. Here, at the beginning of his writing career, we discover Joseph Hergesheimer as a " real " artist; he is going to bring his

lovely characters to ruin—or, as he himself phrases it, be
" a merchant in unhappy endings." He doesn't believe
in the power of the human will to master circumstance,
and he doesn't think it matters much anyway. " I didn't
much believe in the triumph or importance of the
individual." What is the origin of this curse laid upon
the leisure class, an evil spell binding them, so that they
can do nothing but go down with mournful dignity to
their ruin?

And then " Cytherea," a picture of the fashionable free-
spending set, moved from West Chester to Long Island
as a matter of courtesy to Dorothy's folks. These people
live, not by producing wealth, but by speculating in paper
titles to wealth; therefore they have no creative purpose,
and no moral resistance, and corruption gnaws in their
bones. A young stock-gambler, bored with his own wife,
conceives a passion for his friend's wife, and runs away
to Cuba with her and sees her die amid tropical horrors,
corresponding to those in her own soul. A familiar
enough theme, but with a new feature derived from Mr.
Hergesheimer's custom of gazing at articles of furniture
and *objets d'art*, and writing his stories around them.
Perhaps it was Christmas time, and one of Dorothy's
friends had sent her a " kewpie " doll, one of those comic
figures that are set up on mantles in the nursery; anyhow,
the hero of this novel brings home a painted doll and gazes
at it until the creature becomes Cytherea, the ancient
Paphian goddess of sex licence, and he falls under her spell.
This is what is called " high art " in the present-day high-
art world. And don't think it is meant with any humour
—no, we are standing at the tip-top of the tallest ivory
tower in America, and being as solemn as ever we know
how. On the cover of the " Dower House " book we
encounter an opinion from the very highbrow *Saturday
Review,* calling it a " stately book "; and that is the word
to describe Mr. Hergesheimer and his reputation. That
is how he takes himself; to my friend George Sterling he
said, " I am as big a man as Dreiser."

And then " Balisand," the story of a landed gentleman of Maryland during the revolutionary war; here again is " stateliness " to the *n*th power, and as usual written around an article of furniture. Under an illustration in the " Dower House " book you find this caption : " The walnut sideboard, inlaid with long conch-shells in apple-wood, had rare brasses stamped with an Ionic temple. It bore Philadelphia and Georgian silver and a shameless cocktail shaker." It was gazing at this last *objet de joie* that generated the story of Richard Bale of Balisand. We see him in the opening chapter getting elaborately drunk; he is drunk in gentlemanly and aristocratic fashion most of the way through, until he is killed in gentlemanly and aristocratic fashion in a duel over a woman. When I read this novel, I said to a friend, " This Hergesheimer is an eighteenth-century Tory." My friend, a victim of the " art for art's sake " bunk, insisted that the book might be a literary exercise. But now we don't have to dispute any more, Mr. Hergesheimer has settled the matter in his spiritual confession. " Politically, I discovered, writing ' Balisand,' I was a Federalist; a party soon discredited, and—or for this era—completely lost."

He goes on to tell us what he likes in life : " privilege and the exercise of privilege "; " pleasantness and security "; " time to choose neckties "; " a room with a graceful Hepplewhite table, and on it a box of Cabañas cigars—Tabacos Del Almurezo—and Balkan cigarettes "; " a measure of dry gin in a glass with British ginger beer, and ice, and a few drops of the juice of a lime." Such are the tastes of a gentleman of letters. But persons who have not sense enough to share such tastes do not need to worry; they are " in no peril from any effort on my part to extend their joys." No propaganda, you see!

But these joys cost real money, and so Mr. Hergesheimer takes a trip to the fountain-head of real money in the arts, and writes a series of articles for Colonel Lorimer, describing life among the movie stars in language of the most top-lofty stateliness. All in the sacred cause of high art

we learn how Mr. Lasky ties his necktie, and how Mr.
Goldwyn's car is upholstered, and how the valet at the
Ambassador looks at the red suspenders which Mr. Knopf
gave to Mr. Hergesheimer; we are taken the round of
luncheons and dinners, and meet the exquisite young
" shapes in light " in their homes, and gossip with them
and play cribbage, and in all my reading of the literatures
of seven languages and four thousand years, I cannot recall
any artist lending his fancy language to the glorifying of
more empty vanity and pretence. The climax comes in
the home of one of these money-stuffed dolls; the spell of
Cytherea begins to steal over us, and we sit lost in it, until
the beautiful " shape in light " asks what is the matter,
and we reply, " I was just thinking what in the name of
God I'd say if I happened to be in love with you." To
this the " shape " replies, " Don't be silly," and we agree
with all our heart.

The ivory tower artist goes back to Dower House and
Dorothy, and we leave him in the domestic scenes he has
told us about. " On the wide blue rug of the dining-room
walnut and, in the morning sunlight, the engaging
shadows of the fiddle-back chairs, made a very pleasant
pattern against the blanched walls." This delightful
picture may be compared with a paragraph from an
address delivered by Mr. Karl de Schweinitz, secretary of
the Family Society of Philadelphia, a charity organization.
" Of the thousand families studied in December (1926)
many lacked what are the necessities of modern city life.
There were 387 that had no bath-tub, while another 230
were obliged to share a tub with one or more other
families. Less than half of the thousand families had
toilets in their houses. One hundred and ninety-one
families shared a toilet indoors with one or more families;
324 families had outside toilets and 42 families were obliged
to share an outside toilet with other families. There were
actually 60 families that did not have running water in the
house."

Our ivory tower artist describes for us his bedroom, in

which he makes use of the brocaded pyjamas of burnt orange and cerulean and glass green. He says: " The bed in the curly maple room had a canopy like a film, a suspended tracery of frost; and under it many delicate and beautiful women had slept . . . cooled in the white silence of winter." And against that lovely sentence let us set one from an article in the *Survey*, December 15, 1925, by Dr. I. M. Rubinow, director of the Jewish Welfare Society of Philadelphia : " The working-man's apartment in Philadelphia is not an apartment at all, but only two or three rooms sublet without any necessary adjustment for a separate decent family existence, for it has no private bathing or toilet facilities and very frequently no separate water supply."

CHAPTER XX

THE CHARM-POACHER

THE moral content of ivory tower art consists of cruelty and sensuality; the former deriving from the fact that the artist repudiates the brotherhood of man, and the latter from the fact that he repudiates the comradeship of woman. There are two uses for women in the ivory tower—first, to sweep and dust and scrub the floors, and second, to entertain the master by the exercise of that mystical thing he calls " charm." The worst enemy of ivory tower life is boredom, and this puts a heavy task on the charmers; a great many are needed, and they have to work desperately to keep their charms active with lipsticks and scented extracts in slender violet or green vials from Paris. With the best of efforts they are unable to equal the charming of newer and fresher rivals, and so we have tragedies, which afford themes for splendid art works by the next generation of ivory tower dwellers.

It is notorious that a few women are not content with either function, the dusting-sweeping-scrubbing, or the lip-stick-scented-extracts-from-Paris-charming. These women insist upon having something to do with their own destinies, and they are called " shrews," and are the especially bane of ivory tower artists; the condition of being entangled with one of them affords the basis for the comedies of ivory tower life. The artist who is so unlucky as to have his tower seized by a shrew is obliged to flee from her tongue, and he wanders over the world, looking for some charm belonging to some other man, which the wandering artist can steal, because the other man is obliged to be away from home, earning money to pay for the lip-sticks and scented extracts from Paris.

The artist thus flits like a bee from charm to charm, and has a gaily impudent formula which expresses his attitude, " I'll try anything once." Afterwards he can put it into a novel, and live for a lifetime on the royalties; his method of getting something for nothing represents the dearest wish of every member of the leisure classes, and so their favourite fiction deals with charm-poachers.

Eight years ago a clever writer published the life-history of a charm-poacher by the name of " Jurgen." I don't know just how it happened, no doubt some friends of the author called the attention of the anti-vice society of New York to the book, and the publisher was arrested, and the price went up to twenty dollars a copy. The result was that every college undergraduate of any literary pretensions made it the aim of his young life to get " Jurgen " and sit up all night with it, and start trying anything once the following night. So it has come about that James Branch Cabell is the hero and idol of ninety-nine per cent. of our young intelligentsia, and his ivory tower in Richmond, Virginia, almost overtops that of Mr. Hergesheimer.

This son of a distinguished old Virginia family earned his living for many years as a genealogist; that is to say, he was employed to search out or invent ancient lineages and construct family-trees for purse-proud snobs. This has given him inventiveness, pliability of mind, and intimacy with ancient documents and titles; as a fiction-writer he has employed these qualities in the construction of a mythology so plausible that you can hardly tell it from the real—in fact I never did make sure how much of the Jurgen legend is found in the encyclopædia and how much is cabellous. Jurgen wanders far, and many strange experiences befall him, and for a while you are puzzled as to what it is all about; but soon you discover the key, and after that it is all simple : there is a male generative organ, and a female generative organ, and the former approaches the latter, and that is all that ever happens in the Cabell ivory tower, and all you need to know about the fiction, mythology, history, philosophy, art and Episcopal religion of the gentleman in Richmond, Virginia.

I have friends who know Mr. Cabell, and report him as an amiable person, and protest against the vehemence of my loathing for his books. It is not considered good form for radical writers to object to obscenity, for fear of giving aid to the censor. Because you don't want to have your opponents hit over the head by a policeman's club, it is assumed that you make no opposition to them whatever, but take a flabby attitude on moral questions, granting anybody's right to teach anything without rebuke. At risk of numbering myself among the reactionaries, I rise to say that all life is a series of acts of choice, and that according as we choose wisely or otherwisely, we have happiness or suffering, for our innocent posterity as well as for ourselves. That is the meaning of morality; and while scientific progress will alter our choice, nothing will do away with the need of choosing, or the importance of choosing right. The fact that we abolish the policeman's club implies that we intend to make all the more vigorous use of other forces; to wage what William Blake calls " moral fight " in favour of wise and sound life-choosing.

Therefore I give my opinion, that " Jurgen " is one of the most depraved and depraving books ever published in America. It is a long jeering, not merely at marriage, but at love, and every notion of loyalty and honour in love. Jurgen's formula, " I will try anything once "—meaning, of course, I will have sexual relations with any woman once—has had eight years to be thoroughly booklegged among the college youth of America; and I am moved to wonder how many thousands of lads have been caused to suffer atrocious torments from gonorrhœal infection, or to spend their later years in wheel-chairs as a result of syphilitic infection.

I write this, and my friend and biographer, Floyd Dell,

who is reading the proofs, is moved to violent protest. He thinks " there are so many other more moving and realistic persuasions to sexual intercourse "; also that " such books actually take the place of overt action for the people who read them, as Omar's verses take the place of booze." My answer is that of course a great many book-people do lose the habit of action, but surely not all. I have known a number of " booze-fighters " who quoted Omar with genuine fervour. Of course it is not true that an art-work inspires every person to action every time; nevertheless, it is true that art-works are one of the great sources of human action, and have been so recognized by all who wished to incite to action. To say that people can be taught to ridicule true love without ever being led to practise false love, seems to me to overlook the most elementary facts of psychology.

It happens that Floyd Dell is not a worshipper of Cabell's art. But others are, and these fly into a rage with me. " Jurgen " is a priceless work of literature, they tell me; so charmingly written, so witty and sophisticated—surely that makes a difference! My answer is, it makes just as much difference as does the fact that a rattlesnake has the scales on its back arranged in pretty patterns, or that the teeth and claws of a tiger are of ivory whiteness and grace-fully curved. You know exactly how much difference that makes to you, when you find the rattlesnake or the tiger in your home.

CHAPTER XXI

THE TATTOOED NOVELIST

THE fundamental fact to bear in mind concerning capitalist culture is that it maintains a large class of people in luxurious idleness; the cream of labour's product is skimmed off and fed to this class, which renders no service whatever. It is not merely the number of these people, but the fact that they represent the goal of aspiration for the rest, and so what they do and say and think becomes the standard. Capitalist art is an art made for parasites, and exists by glorifying and defending parasitism; it mirrors the most worthless elements in society, and serves to increase the vices upon which it feeds. Our fashions in clothes, for example, are furnished to us by the keepers of French mistresses; whatever these blasé persons find alluring is what our wives and daughters will wear in the coming season—our wives and daughters would rather be dead than behind the times. Or take our moving pictures —what goes into them is decided by the keepers of mistresses in Hollywood; these financially and sexually potent gentlemen put their favourites upon the screen, to display their " charm "—with the result that a large part of our school children are set to acting like little harlots.

The novel is one of the principal channels through which the ideals and manners of " smart " society—that is to say, the idle and wasteful part of the community— are fed to the masses. Every stenographer and telephone girl wants to read the " latest thing "—meaning the newest bit of depravity which some clever brain has devised to amuse the chatterers at fashionable tea-parties. Each season's sensation must be more *outré* than the last; we are more bored, and it takes more to shock us. A generation ago " Sister Carrie " was suppressed because it showed a man and a woman living together without marriage. To-day it is " The Captive " which is suppressed, because it shows two women living together without marriage. Ten years after being suppressed, every such book is a " classic," and its standards are taken as a matter of course by all enlightened persons.

I have in my hands a publisher's circular, sent me three years ago by my friend, George Sterling; on the margin is written, in George's round even hand, " Can you imagine this bird? " The circular quotes an article by Burton Rascoe entitled " Personality Plus," dealing with the author of an ultra-fashionable novel, " The Blind Bow-Boy." This author possesses, we are told, " a bland and saturnine countenance which lights up into a grimace of merriment now and then, showing widely separated teeth. He is tall, white-haired, youngish, with a head that inclines forward from erect shoulders, and a nervous way of moving his head in intermittent slight jerks when he is talking. He has a disconcerting way of looking very intently at a person to whom he has just been introduced and asking him some unexpected question or making some remark for which there is no ready rejoinder. His own repartee is deliberate but acid and witty or sombre and unctuous, according to his mood "—and so on, until you have had enough.

Three years have passed, and this " bird," to use George's irreverent phrase, has become the latest fashion in elegant perversity. The copy of " The Blind Bow-Boy " which lies before me is marked " Seventh Large Edition." It is published by Mr. Knopf, who puts up the money for my friend Mencken's war on prohibition, and who gave Mr. Hergesheimer his red suspenders in Paris. Higher than such a publisher no novelist can climb, so let us see how to please him.

First detail : write all your dialogues without quotation marks. Everybody else uses them, so this will make you different.

Second detail : look up in a big dictionary about fifty words that you never heard before. Thus, *psittacus* is the Latin word for parrot, therefore *psittaceous* means parrot-like. And *dehiscens* is the Latin word for gaping open, so you refer quite casually to the duke's *dehiscent* jaw. It will take you half an hour to find fifty such words, and another half-hour to work them into your manuscript. This alone ensures you permanent fame, because language is made to conceal thought, and the purpose of art is to show the artist's superiority.

Third detail : take a walk down Fifth Avenue and stop in the highest-priced beauty-shop, and note the French names on the bottles of cosmetics and perfumes. Stop at a jeweller's and a curio-dealer's, and learn the latest fads —all this for your lady's boudoir. Get a *couturière* to give you the names of members of her trade in Paris—or make up the names, it doesn't matter, so long as they are French. Get the names of a dozen writers of cultured indecency like yourself, so that you may describe your heroine's reading-table, and have her sweep the fashionable volumes to the floor with a gesture of elegant boredom.

Now you are ready, except that you need an unusual name—Campaspe, let us say—oh, splendid! And a plot? Let a father launch his innocent young son in the world with unlimited money, and a collection of the most depraved companions who can be found for him. Why a father should do this is obviously a mystery, and the adventures of the youth will provide no end of innocent fun. The super-elegant Campaspe, the mother of two children, takes her fashionable male friends for a motor-ride to Coney Island, and they bring home a lady snake-charmer, and in the course of the evening the snake-charmer is discovered in bed with one of the fashionable male friends, and the hostess, of course, is glad to know that her friends are making themselves at home. The

English duke with the *dehiscent* jaw remarks, in the presence of the ladies, that if he invited to his theatre-party all the people he slept with, the theatre would not hold them. When we read things like this, we know we are among the very *crême de la crême*; seven large editions will not be enough, and the great capitalist literary organs will not be able to find words to praise such delicately perfumed excrement.

And then " The Tattooed Countess "—a title alone worth seven more editions. Carl Van Vechten, the author of these master-works, was raised in a small city of Iowa; a terrible place, as seen by a music-critic on a great metropolitan newspaper. Back in Iowa people object to promiscuous cohabitation, and so Mr. Van Vechten seeks to acquaint them with the urbanity and freedom of Europe, where a rich society lady, daughter of a banker and widow of a count, may live the life of a *dame galante*, having as many lovers as she wishes, of all ages and occupations and stations in life. This " tattooed countess " comes back to her home-town in Iowa, her heart having been broken by a recent passionate love-affair with a strolling opera tenor, who wanted nothing but to get as much of her money as he could and spend it on a younger mistress. Through the eyes of this Countess Nattorrini we see the horrors of our American crudity, and watch a charming lady of fifty teach the graces of Europe to a new lover—seventeen years of age! Gertrude Atherton, reviewing this book, hailed the arrival of a great novelist; but she had to admit that the hero struck her as " a trifle too young to inspire tumult in even an elderly and predatory countess." But the reviewer adds, " as no one agreed with me, doubtless this may be a purely personal prejudice." Thus does age abdicate to youth, and moral standards crumble. Anything to keep up with the times —even a tattooed novelist!

And then " Nigger Heaven "; a story of the coloured folks of Harlem, who are now supplying America's requirements in the two arts of music and dancing. The mulatto heroine of this novel might have stepped out of a novel by Louisa Alcott, so good and pure she is; except for that singular penchant, shared by all the Van Vechten ladies, for reading the literature of elegant perversity. Mary Love is a librarian, and labours to improve the literary tastes of the elevator boys and waitresses of the city; but alas, they prefer Zane Grey and Harold Bell Wright to Aldous Huxley and Cabell and Cocteau and Proust and Morand. At the end of the story the elevator boys are still elevating and the waitresses are still waiting, while the hero, who has adopted Mary Love's literary tastes, is shooting bullets into another negro in a drunken café row. So maybe this is a novel with a moral purpose—to warn people against reading Aldous Huxley and Cabell and Cocteau and Proust and Morand—and Van Vechten!

Just recently our literary " bird " flits to Hollywood—following the prevailing fashion for birds of fine feather—and duplicates the performance of Joseph Hergesheimer among the " shapes in light." He stops at the Ambassador, our most fashionable hotel—" Everybody stops at the Ambassador," he tells us, and I mention it for the benefit of my wobbly friends, when next they are released from San Quentin; they can get a very good room and bath for only ten dollars a day. The lady stars gather to exhibit their charms, and our fashionable author scatters adjectives over the pages of " Vanity Fair ": " the joyous childlike . . . the effulgent orchidaceous . . . the gay and dangerously attractive . . . the saucy . . . the blond . . . the barbaric and sullenly splendid . . . the fragile nunlike . . . the wistful . . . the dashing insouciant . . . the amazing . . . the incomparably charming . . . the dark and lovely . . ." All of which fills me with grief for my lost opportunities. Here I have been living near Hollywood for twelve years; I have been there not less than a hundred times, and met not less than two score of the lady stars of the screen; and out of all those meetings I did not get one single thrill, nor one single idea worth putting into fancy language!

CHAPTER XXII

THE BOOKLEGGERS

THERE are scores of other ivory towers we might visit; there are hundreds of packages of delicately perfumed excrement we might sample, at two-fifty per package. But enough excrement is surely as good as a feast.

What is to be done? Some people say, put the venders of indecent books in jail. They are trying it in Boston —and turning the book-trade into a mail-order business. If they keep it up they may drive it underground entirely, like the liquor traffic. But the problem is more difficult in the case of booklegging, because you can only drink liquor once, but a book can be read by a hundred college boys, and will be, if it gets enough police-advertising.

Moreover, experience proves that when you get a censor, you get a fool, and worse yet a knave, pretending to be a guardian of morality, while acting as a guardian of class greed. In Boston they have barred " Elmer Gantry " —because it offends the clergy. We have had a censorship of moving pictures for years, and has it ever barred elegant and luxurious vice, or the preaching of mammon-worship on the screen? No, but it barred " The Jungle " from Chicago, on the express grounds that it injured a leading Chicago industry. Pennsylvania conducts a systematic political censorship, and will not permit you to show an employer who is unkind to his workers. (As I revise these proofs, they have just barred " The Jungle.") In Berkeley, the home of the University of California, they banned Mary Pickford's " Rosita " because it showed a king of Spain who was dissolute. The Better Films Committee explained matters in the Berkeley *Gazette*:

" Plays which belittle offices of authority are incentives for radicalism."

As a " radical," I affirm the futility of plasters on a cancer. You can never stop the writing and selling of depraved books, so long as you permit the existence of an idle rich class, willing to pay unlimited sums of money for the only kind of amusement it can understand. Depraved literature is a symptom, not a cause, and has accompanied the decadence of every great empire in history. Read the " Banquet of Trimalchio," by Petronius, director-general of the imperial pleasures of Nero, and called the " arbiter elegantiæ "; here is ivory tower art in full flower, every element of Cabell and Van Vechten in a story nineteen hundred years old. They had it in Alexandrian Greece, in Byzantium, and in Nineveh and Babylon before that, you may be sure. These and a thousand other empires were destroyed by the combination of luxury at the top and poverty at the bottom; the same combination which is working now in America, with the speed of a racing-car as compared with an ancient bullock-cart.

You can prove this thesis by history, and also you can prove it by psychology. Not one human being in a thousand has the moral stamina to do hard work when he doesn't have to; and here are tens of thousands of people who have never worked, and never will work so long as they are permitted to own the means of life of others. They have been parasites from the formative years of childhood; they have had servants to wait upon them and deprive them of initiative; and now they live, each one a little king or queen, surrounded by flatterers trying to get easy money from them, studying their weaknesses, and persuading them that they are wonderful and great. How many children can grow up sound and strong in such an environment? Read the history of princes!

The rich nourish their own glory, and bring into being a culture in their own image. Just as an individual prince is fawned upon by courtiers, so a privileged class

is coddled by a literature and art of snobbery, such as
I have shown in my studies of Mrs. Humphry Ward and
Henry James and Robert W. Chambers and Gertrude
Atherton and Booth Tarkington and Rupert Hughes and
Elinor Glyn and Wallace Irwin and Joseph Hergesheimer.
And what is that swarm of tame writers Colonel Lorimer
has gathered about him, but the courtiers who danced
attendance on the Grand Monarque and sang his praises?
Louis, who said, " I am the State," went about on red-
heeled shoes and carried a jewelled staff; while Colonel
Lorimer has a mahogany desk and a purring limousine
with a chauffeur in uniform, and says, " I am Culture,"
and all the choir of authors reply, " Yea, sire."   Their
fiction tells him what a wonderful world he has built and
what a marvellous great dog he is.   " I ha' buried many
bones, tho' my ageing hide do itch."

And then, the second generation, and the third—raised
in the purring limousines, and waited on by lackeys in
livery.   The fathers have made big business so perfect
that it runs itself, with only a little oiling, attended to by
competent executives; the golden flood of profits pours in,
and the children have only to spend it.   They have no
restraints—who shall restrain a multi-millionaire?   Will
it be the teachers—the fawning sycophants who have
portrayed themselves in " The Goose-step " and " The
Goslings "?   Will it be the press, which has made the
millionaires into gods, so that when they appear on the
street their lives are endangered by mobs of people
seeking to get near them?   Will it be the police?   When
a millionaire gives an order, the law bows down and hits
its forehead on the ground.

There is a great rich newspaper proprietor in California
who was recently rumoured to have shot and killed a
moving-picture director in a quarrel over a mistress.   I
am told on good authority that it never happened; but
a great many people believed it, and here is the point :
I have heard scores of men discuss the case—no radicals,
but leading men of affairs, journalists, doctors, lawyers,

merchants—and I have yet to meet a single one who did not take it as a matter of course that such a man would be immune to punishment. The career of this man, a child of vast wealth, shows all that you need to know about hereditary privilege as a destroyer of morality. He is keeping a leading movie star as his mistress, and featuring her in luxury plays, and using his chain of newspapers to exalt and glorify her. All members of the ruling class in California know about it, and most of them wish they could do likewise.

The children of the rich run wild, and each new batch outdoes the last. It takes only ten years to make a generation now, and when you are thirty, you are a dead one. Read Gertrude Atherton's " Black Oxen," and see her horrified picture of a flapper; and then see Gertrude Atherton herself suddenly abdicating her judgment before a tattooed novelist. Maybe, after all, it isn't so bad for a fifty-year-old female *rouée* with a title and a fortune to cohabit with a seventeen-year-old boy!

There are thousands of such female *rouées* in our society. You can see them in the luxurious hotels, white-haired old grandmothers dancing all night with their backs half naked. Here in California they have cabins in the canyons to which they motor with boys out of the high schools. Between their visits to the hairdressers and the facial surgeons these up-to-date grandmothers want something to pass the time with, so they command authors to entertain them, and the authors jump, just like the hairdressers and the facial surgeons; the work is so easy and the pay so princely. Thus comes the literature of Cabell and Van Vechten and Morand and Cocteau and Aldous Huxley and Michael Arlen. And it will go on to new extremes; there are still many forms of unnatural vice which have not been exploited in best-sellers; and if the Boston censorship spreads over the rest of the country, the publishers will move to Paris, and you will see book-fleets hovering thirty miles out from the ports of Boston and New York and San Francisco and Los Angeles.

CHAPTER XXIII

THE EX-MUCKRAKERS

ROME had Juvenal, as well as Petronius; and in the same way there are writers in America serving as antibodies to the poisons of plutocracy. Some, like Virgil in Rome, yearn back to the good old days of the founding fathers; others are merely muddled, groping blindly; a few are clear-sighted. As we set out to study them, make note of this fact at the outset, we part company with the great magazines, with circulations up in the one or two and a half millions. No more shall we present walnut sideboards to Colonel Lorimer, no more shall we stop at the Ambassador and exercise our vocabulary upon the screen beauty parade. From now on we have to live on our book royalties, with here and there an article in highbrow or radical papers.

The last writer I can recall who was able to publish in a big popular magazine any hint that there might be something wrong with the American plutocracy, was Winston Churchill. We left him in 1910, so let us glance at his later career, and then at some other veterans of those muckraking days. Mr. Churchill wrote a novel, " The Inside of the Cup," actually troubling the conscience of his Episcopal Church, which had not turned over in its slumbers since Charles Kingsley died. I was sick just then with the long agony of the Lawrence strike, and I remember writing a letter to Mr. Churchill; sitting up till three or four o'clock in the morning, pouring out my eloquence in an effort to persuade him to deal with a great mass strike. He replied that I myself was the person to do it; as if the Episcopal Church would listen to the author of " The Profits of Religion "!

But I must have made some impression on this dignified and conscientious gentleman; for three or four years later appeared " The Dwelling Place of Light "; a novel with scenes laid in a New England mill-town, and a strike for its culmination. But alas, it was a serial for the *Cosmopolitan Magazine*, written down to the Hearst level. A stenographer, of good family, of course, though fallen into reduced circumstances, and how she was seduced by her employer—all the anguish of a great strike serving for a picturesque background to such a theme! I think Mr. Churchill must have been made ashamed, for ten years have passed, and he has not published a novel since.

The other day I wrote, asking him to tell me why, if it was not a secret; and he answered that it was a secret from himself as well as from me. I suspect that means he has had some kind of religious experience, reducing the importance of worldly affairs in his mind. I can understand that; I too was brought up in the Church of Good Society, and carried the bishop's train in the stately ceremonials; I too have had magic hands laid upon my head, and magic formulas pronounced over it. Also, I realize that we don't know very much about this universe; we walk, as it were, upon the quaking top of a volcano. But I take my stand upon the conviction that whatever gods may control our destinies, it will not displease them that men should cease to slaughter one another, and to rob one another of the fruits of toil.

We left Robert Herrick, a university professor, writing novels full of keen insight into the faults of his country. He is still doing it, in the same spirit of grave and rather mournful despair. He has no hope; but he is not among the academic ones who hold a vested interest in pessimism, and are ready, like Paul Elmer More, to bite you if you venture to suggest that man may some day master his fate. Robert Herrick would be glad of a faith, but he has no knowledge of the labour movement, the embryo of the new society. His last novel, "Chimes," is the spiritual confession of a professor. He gently rebukes "The Goose-step" as too extreme, but I laughed as I read his novel—I am well content with his picture of capitalist-endowed education!

And then Edith Wharton. The war hit this vigorous mind a hard blow; she got two doses of patriotism, first French, and then American. Now she has gone back to writing novels about smart society, but the sting is gone out of them. Is it that we are no longer startled to hear about idleness, waste and wantonness among the rich? Or is it that Edith Wharton herself has grown used to the spectacle, and tired and hopeless? Undoubtedly the latter; she is sixty-five years old, and it is not so easy to swim against the current. The other day she handed down her opinion upon the best-seller of the day, "Gentlemen Prefer Blondes," "I have just been reading what seems to me to be the great American novel." For the benefit of those who read this book ten years from now I explain that "Gentlemen Prefer Blondes" is a witty and cynical sketch of the high-priced young harlots of our international bourgeoisie. It isn't a novel, and to call it "great" represents an abdication of judgment hardly to be believed of the woman who wrote "The House of Mirth."

Who else from those old muckraking days? Ernest Poole wrote "The Harbour," a really beautiful novel of the class struggle in New York; now he writes amiable and unimportant stories of the domestic problems of the well-to-do. Herbert Quick wrote a noble fighting book, "The Broken Lance," the story of a rebel clergyman; and then he toned down and produced a three volume chronicle of Iowa, apologizing for the graft and waste he had formerly denounced.

And then Brand Whitlock, who wrote the best story of all, "The Turn of the Balance." Nobody else has portrayed so completely the mixture of graft and cruelty which calls itself " criminal law " in capitalist America; not even " An American Tragedy " has a more heart-shaking climax. And now what? The one-time radical mayor became ambassador to Belgium, and a popular hero with strings of titles and decorations; he comes home and settles down to write about a wealthy carriage manu-facturer of the Middle West who renews his youth with a pretty little milliner, but has the misfortune to be caught by the fire department. That is " J. Hardin and Son," and it is pathetic enough, but where is the old vision? And then " Uprooted," about the elegant idlers whom Ambassador Whitlock watched in Europe; but what has happened to make them so dignified and so important, both to their creator and to us?

The spiritual transformation is revealed in one sentence of the book, where the author turns aside from his story for a sneer at the French workers: " hangdog raga-muffins were slouching on the benches, reading in Socialist newspapers of the happy time to come when all men everywhere would knock off work and live on the stock on hand." I wrote a letter to the author of that sentence, asking him to justify it. I have been reading Socialist papers, magazines and books both here and abroad, for twenty-five years, and have never seen a hint of such an idea, and I challenged the ex-ambassador to show such a line in any Socialist publication. The fact is that the Socialists, in France, as everywhere else, seek exactly the opposite goal, a world in which it is impossible for anyone to live without working. But in Brand Whitlock's novel are portrayed a group of people no one of whom is doing any useful work—with the possible exception of the hero, who paints portraits of wealthy idlers. Surely these are the persons " living on the stock on hand! " Needless to say, the ex-ambassador did not reply to this letter. What could he have said?

CHAPTER XXIV

MUDDLEMENT

I HAVE stated that some of our protestant writers are muddled. I begin with one who is muddlement and nothing else; muddlement not merely by nature but by choice; muddlement as a religion, a philosophy, and an ethical code. " How are you going to understand women when you cannot understand yourself? How are you going to understand anyone or anything? " So Sherwood Anderson asked himself at the age of twelve; and now he is fifty-one, and has asked it in six novels, three volumes of short stories, a collection of poems, a note-book, and two autobiographies.

Eleven years ago I came on a first novel by an unknown writer; a novel which gave me a thrill because it showed real knowledge of poverty and real tenderness for the poor. So few of our magnificent wealthy writers condescend to be aware of poverty—except when they need a contrast to heighten the charms of a plutocratic career. So I wrote a letter to the author of " Windy McPherson's Son," seeking to make a Socialist out of him. He answered, on the letter-head of an advertising firm in Chicago, and we had a little correspondence, from which I quote a few sentences.

" To me there is no answer for the terrible confusion of life. I want to try to sympathize and to understand a little of the twisted and maimed life that industrialism has brought on us. But I can't solve things, Sinclair. I can't do it. Man, I don't know who is right and who

H

wrong. . . . Really, I am tempted to go at you hard
in this matter.   There is something terrible to me in the
thought of the art of writing being bent and twisted to
serve the ends of propaganda . . . Damn it, you have
made me go on like a propagandist.   You should be
ashamed of yourself."

And then came a second novel, " Marching Men," to
make clear to me that I need have no hope of social
understanding from Sherwood Anderson.   Here is the
story of a labour leader who rouses the workers; and for
what?   To march!   Where shall they march?   He
doesn't know.   What shall they march for?   He doesn't
know that.   What is their marching to be understood to
symbolize?   Nobody knows; but march, and keep on
marching—" Out of Nowhere into Nothing," to quote
the title of a Sherwood Anderson short story.

I have never met this writer, but he has told me
everything I need to know.   He began life in poverty;
the critics compare him with the Russians, and the only
way he can account for it is that he was raised on cabbage
soup.   He means this playfully, apparently not realizing
that the thwartings and humiliations of extreme poverty
do actually produce mental disorders in sensitive and high-
strung children, and account for exactly those muddlements
which were the literary stock-in-trade of the victims of
the Tsardom.

Upon the basis of the data in the books, I venture to
psycho-analyse Mr. Anderson, and tell him that he is the
victim of a dissociated personality.   From childhood he
wanted to create beauty, and had to live in a dirty hovel,
upon a supply of cabbages which rowdies had thrown
at his mother's door one night.   Then he had to go
out into the world of hustle and graft, to fight for. a
living; he had to become manager of a paint factory,
without the least interest in that kind of paint.   And all
the while the repressed artist in him sobbed and suffered,
and lived its own subconscious life, and occasionally
surged up to the surface, driving the respectable paint

factory manager to actions which his stenographer and office force considered insane. It drove him to drop the paint job, all of a sudden, right in the middle of the dictating of a letter; it drove him to a nervous breakdown, and the life of a wanderer; it drove him to throw up a first-class advertising job in Chicago; and finally it made him a man of genius, the object of adoration of all those critics who have been fed on warmed-over cabbage soup, and whose test of great literature is that it shall be muddled.

This is the age—I was going to say of Freud, but I correct myself and say, of Freudians. Freud himself is a great pioneer of science; but like many another master, he has raised up a horde of followers who pervert his doctrine in spite of all he can do. We know the swarms of Nietzscheans, who think that the superman is embodied in a big-fisted bully; we know the Whitmanites, who think that genius means brag and bluster and exhibitionism. In the same way there are Freudians, who find the cause of all "complexes" in failure to follow every sexual whim. Freud himself teaches "sublimation," directing the sexual energy into the channels of artistic and intellectual creation. I read his books before any of them had been translated into English, so I have watched this cult from the beginning, and have seen my muddled young friends in Greenwich Village set out on a crusade to "syke" all the married couples they know, and discover that they are suffering from "repressions," and persuade them to a divorce, or at the least a few adulteries.

And so came Sherwood Anderson, right in the Freudian swim; all his characters are victims of dissociation, and always they find the solution of their problem in following a sexual impulse. Civilization is repressed, says our novelist, and he writes a long novel, "Dark Laughter," to show a man and a woman, mentally disordered, and therefore drawn to each other, as happens with all neurasthenics, and discovering in the free, happy laughter

of negroes the state of naturalness they seek.   Mr. Anderson finds about the negroes what Whitman found about
the animals, they do not worry about their sins; and so
his couple go off together, and we are left to assume
that they will be happy.   But I can tell him that they
won't, because I have lived a good part of my life among
neurasthenics—who has not, in modern civilization?—and
I see his two people presently discovering that they have
a complex, due to the fact that one is repressing the other's
nature.

There is a cancer, eating out the heart of our civilization; but no one is permitted to diagnose that cancer,
under penalty of losing his job and social standing.   No
one who understands economic inequality as a cause of
social and individual degeneration is permitted to hold
any responsible post in capitalist society; and so it comes
about that muddlement is the ideal of our intellectuals.
Suppose that Mr. Anderson had written in his letter to
me, " Yes, of course, I see the class struggle.   How could
any clear-sighted man fail to see it?   How could any
honest man fail to report it? "   Would he then have
become the white hope of all the intelligentsia, as he is
to-day?   No indeed!   The way to be a genius of the
Freudian age is to write, " How are you going to understand anyone or anything? "   When the intellectual
reads that, he slaps his leg and cries, " Aha!   Here is
sincerity!   Here is naturalism!   Here is the real,
elemental, primitive, naïve!   Here is a true overflow,
red-hot lava boiling up from the subconscious!   Here is
something Russian!   Here is cabbage soup! "

You laugh, perhaps; people generally laugh when you
state an obvious truth about this crazy world.   But take
the thirteen volumes of Sherwood Anderson and analyse
the characters : men and women who cannot adjust themselves to any aspect of life, cannot live in marriage or
out of it, cannot make love, cannot consummate love,
cannot restrain love, cannot keep from being suspected
of perversity; and always, everywhere, over and over

again, the one repressed artist personality making agonized efforts to state himself in words, saying the same thing over and over, a dozen times on a single page. He tells us that artist's story in " Windy McPherson's Son," and then he tells it, with variations, in " Poor White "; he tells it, full and complete, in " A Story-Teller's Story "; he tells the childhood over again in " Tar," and the married part in " Many Marriages," and again, with changed circumstances, in " Dark Laughter "; and then the philosophy of it in a " Notebook "; and then the short stories—this or that aspect of the same theme. Some of them are great short stories, but I have said to myself, long or short, I have read that story enough times!

CHAPTER XXV

AN AMERICAN VICTORY

Theodore Dreiser is another man who has told us his
own story. In " A Book About Myself," he makes
himself known to us on page one, and we observe that
the child is father to the man. Wandering about the
streets of Chicago, a homeless, jobless, miserable youth,
he reads a newspaper column by Eugene Field, and " this
comment on local life here and now, these trenchant bits
on local street scenes, institutions, characters, functions,
all moved me as nothing hitherto had." That was thirty-
seven years ago, and Dreiser is still interested in the local
life of America; he is interested in life here and now, no
other time or place; he watches " street scenes, institutions, characters, functions," and stores them up in the
notebook of his memory, and when he has a few million
of them, he weaves them into a vast pattern.

He wanted to be a newspaper man; he had no idea
how to begin, but he hung around a newspaper office,
like a poor stray dog, until people got tired of kicking
him out, and finally gave him something to write. So
then he saw America from the inside. " I began to see
how party councils and party tendencies were manu-
factured or twisted or belied, and it still further reduced
my estimate of humanity. Men, as I was beginning to
find—all of us—were small, irritable, nasty in their
struggle for existence." An editor says to him: " Life
is a God-damned, stinking, treacherous game, and nine
hundred and ninety-nine men out of every thousand are

bastards." That is newspaper talk, and that is the
newspaper man's world, in which Theodore Dreiser
spent his formative years.

The men of that world had very few of them what we
call "education"; they had learned reading, writing,
arithmetic, and geography, and then gone to work. They
knew nothing about the past, and had no vision of the
future, no science, no understanding of the causes of
anything. What they knew was the world about them,
its external aspects which they "wrote up" day by day;
when they had "inside" knowledge of anything, it
meant the intrigues and rascalities of men of power,
"bastards" like themselves, except that they had wealth,
or the greed and energy to prey upon the wealthy.
Newspaper offices were dirty, and newspaper men worked
under terrific pressure, with the aid of narcotics and
stimulants; they lived in a blue smoke of nicotine, and
kept a bottle of whisky in their desks, and paid a visit
to the corner saloon every time they left the office.

When you climbed higher, into the magazine world,
and became a managing editor of Butterick publications,
as Dreiser was for many years, you found a world
externally different, but spiritually the same; you had a
clean office, with rugs on the floor and a shiny desk and
a potted palm in the corner, but the members of the staff
were the same "bastards," risen by virtue of their ability
to judge with greater accuracy what the nameless millions
outside would spend their money for. Dreiser possessed
that ability, and might have been a managing editor yet,
but there was something else in him, as in Sherwood
Anderson. But he did not let it wreck him; he bided
his time, and made his mental notes—you will find that
magazine world of fashion in "The Genius." I used
to meet Dreiser in those days, a big silent fellow. I liked
to talk, and he liked to listen.

In his early days he wrote a novel, "Sister Carrie,"
telling the story of a girl of the sort he knew, one who
had no wealth and family prestige to protect her, and who

therefore lived with a man of the business world; it seemed to Carrie quite natural to do that, and also it seemed that way to Dreiser. But the bourgeois world of a generation ago was performing a kind of incantation upon itself, insisting that such things didn't happen; an elderly maiden aunt of Doubleday, Page & Company read this wicked book just after it appeared, and caused the remaining copies to be locked up. Dreiser was poor and unknown and friendless, and might have landed in jail if he had tried to make any protest. So that was the end of " Sister Carrie "—until it became a classic.

A clear-sighted and truth-telling man has to have a tough hide to survive in such a world. As I think Dreiser over, the quality which impresses me is stubbornness. He knows what he wants, and he will wait as many years as necessary, but in the end he will get it. He is like an old bull elephant, shoving his way through a jungle; nothing diverts him, he goes on pushing and pushing. When he gets out, his hide will be scarred and knobby, but he will be the same old elephant.

Dreiser in " An American Tragedy " is exactly the same as in " Sister Carrie." He has had twenty-five years in which to observe " the local street scenes, institutions, characters, functions " of America; and so he knows more detail about them, but he does not understand any better how they came to be, or how they may become otherwise. His heart aches for the waste and suffering, he broods over his characters like a fond mother, excusing them for everything they do—how could they do otherwise? The grim stubbornness which made Theodore Dreiser one of the world's great novelists is too much to be expected of Carrie Meeber and Jennie Gerhardt and Eugene Witla and Clyde Griffiths—they are all weaklings, grist for the inexorable mills of fate.

The philosophy of Dreiser is the same as that of Thomas Hardy. Both of them see human beings as the sport of natural forces never to be comprehended; and the sublimity of both rests upon your willingness to accept their philosophy of moral nihilism. Hardy has choruses of various kinds of spirits and superior beings to explain to us the blind tragedy of the dynasts; but Dreiser serves as his own chorus, his pity and grief is like a monotone of muted strings underneath his narratives of futility and false glory.

I am not quarrelling with this great-hearted writer because he is not a Socialist in the narrow sense. Scientific Socialism is only a part of man's big job of understanding the blind forces of nature and subordinating them to his will. Read a little book by a true scientist, Ray Lankester's " The Kingdom of Man," and learn what is the matter with our world. We have partly suppressed the natural process of selection and elimination of the unfit; and we have either to go on and take rational control of the improvement of human stocks and the environment in which they grow, or else see our culture degenerate and perish. Birth control and eugenics are the merciful ways of eliminating the unfit; while sanitation and hygiene, the socialization of production and the abolition of parasitism, are means of raising the new race. But to Dreiser all this world of science is non-existent; nobody ever heard of it in the newspaper offices where he got his education. The nearest he has come to it is Christian Science, with which the hero of " The Genius " dallies in his period of defeat and despair. Human beings cannot live on pessimism, however nobly felt and eloquently expressed; if they are not permitted to study the science of Professor Lankester, they will adopt that of Mrs. Eddy.

Dreiser is the idol of our young writers to-day; a better divinity than others I have named, for the reason that he has not abdicated to snobbery. He has portrayed both poverty and wealth, and held the balance true; the great magazine world of fashion did not overwhelm him with awe while he lived in it. Now he has a best-seller, and has made two hundred thousand dollars, and that is an American victory. What will he do with it? A cruel joke upon our young intelligentsia, if their big quiet idol were to turn into an old-style Christian preacher!

There are signs of it. "An American Tragedy" is a Sunday-school sermon all complete; the church folks have only to expurgate the story of the seduction, which goes into more detail than is customary in Sunday schools. But everything else is there, the early religious training, the fond mother praying for her wandering boy, the wicked world of wealth and fashion, the primrose path of vice, the pangs of guilt and fear, the temptation and the dreadful crime, the detection and conviction—and then the fond mother with her prayers again, and the clergyman kneeling in the prison, repentance and forgiveness and the everlasting mercy of God. Fifty-six years Theodore Dreiser has had to look at life with his own independent eyes, and report his own original unbiased opinion; and it turns out to be this novel and startling doctrine: " The wages of sin is death! "

CHAPTER XXVI

BOOBUS AMERICANUS

PONDERING how to open this chapter, through some whim of memory I return to the fashion that was taught me in my tender youth. We had, in our homely old college, an institution known as " chapel." At eight-forty-five every morning we assembled in a large hall, to gaze upon a platform decorated by a row of white-haired old gentlemen, the faculty. Our " prexy," an ex-brigadier-general, would read us from an expurgated edition of the Bible, and then a more or less rattled upper classman would be summoned to the platform to pronounce an oration of his own inspired composition. For a week or two in advance he had been coached for the ordeal by an instructor of elocution, who would take his manuscript and mark it here and there on the margin with cryptic initials, " rg " which meant a gesture with the right hand, " lg " which meant a gesture with the left hand, and " gbh " which meant a moment of especial inspiration, signalized by a generous, all embracing gesture with both hands. So we would take our stand upstage centre, with sixteen hundred eyes fixed upon us, and trembling visibly in the knees, and quavering in the voice, we would begin, according to an ancient and immutably established pattern, as follows :

Henry Louis Mencken, one of the most influential and widely-discussed of modern critics, was born in Baltimore, Maryland, on the 12th of September, 1880. He is of German parentage, and was educated in the public schools of his native city, and in the Baltimore Polytechnic

Institute.   He began his career as a journalist, and was for many years connected with the daily which Baltimoreans know as the *Sunpaper*.   He then became editor of the *Smart Set*, and for ten years imparted to that monthly a character unique and *sui generis*.   (We had compulsory Latin for five years at our college, and we always got some of it in.)   He then founded the *American Mercury*, and has built up a large circulation and still wider influence by criticism expressed in a pungent and arresting style——

I get that far, but it doesn't seem right, and at last I realize what is the matter : never during the entire five years of my interment in this venerable college did I hear an oration pronounced upon a subject who was guilty of the vulgarity of being alive.   So that was a false start, and I try again, in the fashion of those pungent and arresting biographical sketches which appear each month between the arsenical green covers.   So :

Upon an overstuffed plush sofa in the reception-room of the fashionable Women's Athletic Club of Los Angeles there sits a short and solidly made gentleman with bright china-blue eyes and the round rosy face of a cherub.   He is about to play the lion at a luncheon in the dining-room, and meantime he is entertaining a small group with a diverting account of the adventures of a Babbitt-hunter in the land of Babbitts.   H. L. Mencken has been making a tour of the South; and when he boarded the train in New Orleans, very much in need of sleep after days of festivities, he discovered that the general passenger agent of the road had telegraphed the district superintendent, and this worthy had notified the conductor of the train and all the station agents on the line, so that hospitality might not cease during any hour of the day or night.   The steward of the dining-car brought pots of steaming coffee, and the " butcher " brought baskets of fruit, and the train conductor brought real Scotch, or so he said, and the Pullman conductor conjured a magical mint-julep, and at every stop there was a local deputation, with flowers and brass bands and beautiful smiling maidens; in short, it was exactly like a presidential campaign tour, except that the victim would rather have been reading a book. His china-blue eyes twinkled with mischief and his rosy face grew apoplectic as he pictured the efforts of a weary editor to close his eyes in slumber while the outside air rang with " Hail to the Chief! " and the door of the compartment had the varnish worn off by tapping knuckles.

The eminent editor had written that he was coming to see me; and I had mentioned the matter to friends, never dreaming the risk I was running. One day the story exploded like a bomb-shell in the newspapers, and after that my telephone was never still. One newspaper announced that I had announced that Mencken was going to address the local Babbitts; and then it printed an interview with the secretary of the local Babbitts, saying that Mr. Mencken wasn't going to address them, and who was Mr. Mencken anyhow? Another paper announced that I was going to make a Socialist out of Mencken, and then came an interview with Mencken *en route*, saying that it was a mistake, he was going to make a drunkard out of me. All the newspaper men I know begged for a seat at that fight when it came off. But it was a poor show; you don't argue with Niagara, and you don't interrupt a circus.

Mencken is in a Berserk rage against stupidity, dullness and sham; he is a whole army, horse, foot, artillery, aviation and general staff all in one, mobilized in a war upon his enemies. He has a spy bureau all over the country, which collects for him illustrations of the absurdities of democracy, and he sorts them out by states, and once a month they appear between the arsenical green covers, and once a year they make a book, " Americana, 1927." If you ask Mencken what is the remedy for these horrors, he will tell you they are the natural and inevitable manifestations of the boobus Americanus. If you ask him why then labour so monstrously, he will say that it is for his own enjoyment, he is so constituted that he finds his recreation in laughing at his fellow-boobs. But watch

him a while, and you will see the light of hilarity die out
of his eyes, and you will note lines of tiredness in his face,
and lines of not quite perfect health, and you will realize
that he is lying to himself and to you; he is a new-style
crusader, a Christian Antichrist, a tireless propagandist
of no-propaganda.

Once I got him to be serious, and he told me the real
basis of his faith, which is liberty; he wishes to abolish
every kind of restriction upon thought and expression, and
to reduce restrictions upon action to the absolute minimum,
those things which are obviously and immediately harmful.
When I suggest that a man who takes alcohol into his
system destroys his hepatic cells, Mencken says to hell with
his hepatic cells; when I tell him that such a man becomes
a dangerous lunatic driving a fast machine on a public
highway, Mencken says get off the highway; when I say
that he destroys the health of his posterity, Mencken says
that is posterity's hard luck.   At least that is the best I
could make of it; he has a tendency to become incoherent
when the subject of prohibition is raised, and it took
several samples of my rich uncle's pre-Volstead stock to
soothe him into rationality again.

He lashes with his powerful language the stupidities of
bureaucrats and the knaveries of politicians.   He declares
that government is " the common enemy of all well-
disposed, industrious and decent men."   I protest to him
that this is a rather sweeping statement; for example, our
government distributes the *American Mercury*, and is it
then " the common enemy of well-disposed, industrious
and decent men "?   He replies—I am quoting from a
written controversy—that the government doesn't want to
distribute the *Mercury*, and wouldn't if it could help it.
But that is obviously no reply, we are discussing a matter
of business, not of psychology, and the fact is that the
government does distribute the *Mercury*, on precisely the
same terms as all other magazines.   I cite the fact that it
issues many postal orders for five dollars each, which the
publishers of Mencken's magazine collect.   He replies that

the government loses most of these orders. I cite the fact that the government will come and save his house if it catches fire, and he answers that fire departments are so inefficient that most fires burn out.

These statements illustrate an unfortunate weakness of our great libertarian crusader, he has very little regard for facts; all he is thinking about is to amuse and startle. He once made a funny newspaper article about me as the man who has believed more things than any other man alive; he managed to compile a plausible list, by including a number of things which I don't believe and never did; also, a number of things which all sensible men believe— including Mencken himself, if you could pin him down; and finally, a few things which I believe because I have investigated them, and which Mencken disbelieves because he is ignorant about them.

For example, fasting. I have published a book setting forth the fact that fasting will cure many diseases. Mencken has never fasted, and has never read a book on the subject—I managed in our correspondence to bring out that fact. I have taken the precaution to fast twenty or thirty times for longer or shorter periods, and I have received letters from thousands of others who have tried it. Since my book appeared, sixteen years ago, many of my contentions have been vindicated by exact scientific research, at the Carnegie laboratories and other places. I offer to my friend Mencken the results of work done at the Hull Biological Laboratory of the University of Chicago, and reported in the *Journal of Metabolic Research*, showing the results of thirty and forty-day fasts upon human beings and dogs, a permanent increase in the metabolic rate of five or six per cent. Inasmuch as decrease in the metabolic rate is one of the phenomena of old age, it follows that the effect of fasting is rejuvenation—which is exactly what I have been asserting for sixteen years. But did Mencken trouble to consult the *Journal of Metabolic Research* before compiling his list of Sinclair absurdities? No indeed, and he didn't consult it afterwards; I am still waiting for him to tell his readers the vitally important facts which have been established about fasting.

Again, I was rebuked in Mencken's review of " Mammonart," for having suggested an identity in the fundamental ideas of Jesus and Nietzsche. That seemed to Mencken the height of absurdity; but he did not give his readers the words I had quoted from Jesus and Nietzsche, which are in substance identical. My friend Haldeman-Julius came forward to rebuke me for disputing with such a Nietzsche authority as Mencken; so pardon me if I mention that Mencken's study of Nietzsche bears the date 1908, while you will find in my " Journal of Arthur Stirling," published in 1903, a complete statement of the Nietzsche philosophy, with translations of many passages.

Liberty, says Mencken. So let me quote him a few words from his great master. " Art thou such a one that can escape a yoke? Free from what? What is that to Zarathustra! Clear shall your eye tell me : free *to* what? " And that is the time when Mencken's eye becomes clouded. The darling and idol of the young intelligentsia has no message to give them, except that they are free to do what they please—which they interpret to mean that they are to get drunk, and read elegant pornography, and mock at the stupidities and blunders of people with less expensive educations. Mencken has " made his school," as the French say; he has raised up a host of young persons as clever as their master, and able to write with the same shillelah swing. For the present, that is all that is required; that is the mood of the time, cynicism, ridicule, and contempt for democratic bungling. But some day the time spirit will change; America will realize that its problems really have to be solved, and that will take serious study of exploitation and wage-slavery, of cooperation and the democratic control of industry—matters concerning which Mencken is as ignorant as any Babbitt-boob.

There lies on my desk his new book, an onslaught upon democracy. In the fly-leaf he has written : " Upton

Sinclair, to make him yell! " And perhaps this is yelling
—judge for yourself. My friend Mencken has made the
discovery that the masses of the people are inferior to
himself; but that political fact was known to every French
marquis of the *ancien régime*.

We agree that we want the wise and competent in
power; the question is, how are they to get there? The
principle of hereditary aristocracy has been given a long
trial, and Mencken omits to tell us where in history's roll
of wars and intrigues and assassinations he finds the ideal
state. At present we have a government based on the
right of active and enterprising capital to have its own
way; under this system the *American Mercury* has built
up a hundred thousand circulation, and the popular editor
is not nearly so discontented as he talks. But meantime
the masses of labour see themselves disinherited and dis-
possessed, and the rumble of their protest grows audible.
Sooner or later my friend Mencken will have to face these
new facts, and choose between the bloody reaction of
Fascism and the new dawn of industrial brotherhood.
Being seven hundred and twenty-three days older than he,
I am going to be his guide and mentor through those
trying times, and he will learn, even while he fusses and
scolds and insists that he won't.

CHAPTER XXVII

THE CRITIC-CASTE

EVERY successful artist becomes host to a number of parasites, the critics who live by telling the public what the artist means, and how and why he is great. The average person is unable to formulate a judgment of an art work; he knows what he likes, of course, but literature is a more serious matter. You have heard the story of the little boy who asked his mother how it happened that all the things that tasted good were bad for you, while those which were good for you were so hard to get down.

Literature, in the capitalist order, is a profession, and like other professions it is concerned to increase its own prestige and emoluments. Do not say that you have a sore throat, says the doctor; come to me and let me tell you that you have follicular pharyngo-tonsilitis, with leucocytosis of the parenchyma and inflammation of the arytenoid cartilage and the lymphoid crypts. In exactly the same way, don't say that the characters in Proust's novels are miserable sex-degenerates; get Henry B. Fuller, a venerable professional of American letters, to tell you that " Sappho and Urania appear as the twin patronesses of Proust's *œuvre* "; or let Anatole France, a venerable professional of French letters, describe Proust as " un Bernardin de Saint Pierre dépravé " and " un Petrone ingénu."

If you join the congregation of the Proust-worshippers, and read these interminable volumes, you will find that the aristocrats of present-day France, like all other decadent groups, have an elaborate code for the conduct of their idle and empty lives: the words they use and the accents they give them, the costumes they consider proper, their manner of lifting an eyebrow at what they disapprove. And the farther the process of their degeneration proceeds, the more remote from reality and common-sense do their standards become; they have to invent finer shades of difference, because there are hordes of Americans, watching them, and having the insolence to publish books of etiquette.

And exactly the same system prevails among the professional highbrows of literature and art. The standards of these critics have no relationship to beauty, kindness, or wisdom; they are a code of artificialities, designed to enable the critic to awe his victims. They lay emphasis upon technique, since that is the aspect of art concerning which the ordinary person seldom thinks; nor indeed does the artist, until his powers have begun to wane. The sophisticated critic accumulates a vast complex of technical and historical knowledge, and overwhelms us with this apparatus of learning, and with his ability to appreciate work in which we can see no sense whatever.

In the days of my youth it was the academic critics who were set over me, and they put me to translating Xenophon and Thucydides, Virgil and Plautus. Then I went on to " post-graduate work," and I remember for two weeks having to struggle through a translation of Ariosto; I am sure I never spent an equal length of time at a more silly occupation. The world war was only fifteen years away, and anyone but a moron could see it coming; and there I sat, dutifully reading elaborate and high-flown descriptions of the efforts of mythological monsters to accomplish rape upon the persons of beautiful maidens of the mediæval Italian nobility!

And when I rebelled, and sought to find out about modern books, there was a learned critic, established in the seat of authority, and equipped to tell me about the living writers of Europe. James Gibbons Huneker was his name, and the august house of Scribner published his essays, in which he discovered a score of new French and Italian and Hungarian poets every year. I don't know how many years he worked at it, but to illustrate his method, let us assume that at a given date he has announced the arrival of one hundred new poets, and is writing an essay hailing number one hundred and one. You then read : " One Hundred and One has the athletic verve of One Hundred, and the vertiginous *élan* of Ninety-Nine, but is lacking in the elegant *insoucience* of Ninety-Eight, and the *méchante diablerie* of Ninety-Seven. He combines the technical *expertise* of Ninety-Six with the atrabiliar fuliginosity of Ninety-Five, and the exotic flair of Ninety-Four "—and so on till you had got back, say to Number Sixty, where you stopped, because the poets prior to that number had most of them died of delirium tremens since their discovery by Huneker ten years previously, and anyhow, old things are a bore. And if you think I am caricaturing a famous critic, just look up one of those old essays, and see how many foreign names he could manage to drag into one paragraph. You didn't learn much about his poets, but you learned a great awe of the critic, and this was the effect the critic had set out to produce.

And now we are in the ivory tower age, and have a swarm of critics who base their judgments upon the Cabell thesis, that the purpose of literature is to find more varied and subtle ways of hinting at the approach of the male and female generative organs. These critics are learned in the lore of a hundred languages, living and dead, and they search the legends and inventions of all time, and compile essays of vast erudition, which are published in our most respectable literary reviews, and it makes me think of the ancient tale about the crowds of people who assembled to marvel at the gorgeous new robes of their queen, and all cried out with admiration and wonder, until suddenly one little boy exclaimed, " Why, the queen is naked! " A little boy critic is urgently needed now, to say, in plain, everyday English, " Why, this is just copulation! "

The various schools of professional *littérateurs* constitute an aristocracy all their own, a critic-caste. They are not content with looking down upon the common herd, they even affect to look down upon the rich and mighty of the earth, who have not been able to spend several years in the cafés of Paris, learning to pronounce the names of eccentric poets from two-score nationalities, and to discover the hidden rhythms of the newest *cénacle* of free verse tricksters. Or maybe the critic has been to Ireland, and discovered a series of epics about Cuchulain, written by a modern poet in ancient Erse; or maybe it is a *commedia dell' arte* in Sicily, or a theatre movement in the ghettos of Warsaw, or a painter of primitives from Tahiti, or of geometrical lines labelled " Nude Coming Downstairs." Anything, so long as it is sufficiently difficult to understand ! Many years ago I remember in the *New Age* of London, a literary explorer returning from a tour of South America with a whole string of poetical scalps; a new culture, outdoing anything previously known in the world, but unfortunately all in Spanish, and too exquisite to be translated !

There lies before me a sumptuous volume, bound in orange-yellow cloth : " Emerson and Others," by Van Wyck Brooks. The public is invited to pay three dollars for this work of the bookmaker's art, and apparently does so, because it is one of the successes of the critical season, the leading reviews all devote columns and pages to praising it. It is a perfect example of the highbrow school, fastidious and aloof, comparing with literature as chiselled marble to the living body. Mr. Brooks fights the battles of privilege with the weapons of disdain; while at the same time maintaining an elaborate pose of liberalism, and a serenity so lofty that it scorns to be aware of opposition.

One of the other " others " in this volume is my unfortunate self; my novels are disposed of in half a dozen devastating pages. I am the betrayer of the working classes, because I tempt them into self-pity, and hatred of their oppressors.   Hatred of oppressors tends to place you more at the oppressors' mercy, says Mr. Brooks—but does not condescend to explain this cryptic utterance.   As proof of my evil influence he contrasts the labour movements of America and Europe.   The former, which has been exposed for so long to my writings, is weak, its members being " intellectual and moral infants," while the movements in Europe are, " in comparison, strong . . . because the masses of individuals that compose them are, relatively speaking, not intellectual and moral infants, but instructed, well-developed, resourceful men."

This essay was first published in the *Freeman* six years ago; and at that time I supplied to Mr. Brooks the facts, which happen to be exactly the opposite of what he states. The novels of Upton Sinclair named by him—" King Coal," " Jimmie Higgins," and " 100%," have had very little circulation among the workers of America, but the " instructed, well-developed, resourceful men " of the labour movements of Europe have devoured them.   These novels have appeared serially in scores of Socialist, Communist and labour papers, and in book-form have been best-sellers in French, German, Italian, Dutch, Swedish, Norwegian, Finnish, Yiddish, Polish, Czechish, Slavic and Ukrainian.   Literally scores of editions have been published in Russia, they have toured the country as stage-plays, and moving pictures have been made of them.

These facts I supplied to Mr. Brooks; and what attention did he pay to them?   He waited six years, and then reprinted his false thesis without altering a single essential word!   And that is what passes for critical authority in America!

CHAPTER XXVIII

SPEAKING TO GOD

So far we have discussed the novelists and the critics of capitalist America. There remain the poets, and I have to begin by confessing that while I have read a thousand or two of modern novels and critical works, I have read only a hundred or two of poets. I like to get some return for the trouble of running my eyes over printed lines of type. When I read a novel by any of the new men, I get at least some facts about the world I live in; but in a new poet I find a creature spinning a cocoon out of his own juices. Sometimes he imitates the poets of the past, figuring out ways to vary their phrases; or else he makes a desperate effort to be different, and succeeds only in being odd. This is an age of material glory, and the first condition of true poetic impulse is revolt. But there is no way for rebel poets to get a comfortable living, and nobody in America is willing to live any other way; so, with two or three exceptions that I can think of, our rebel poets are dead, or silent, or turned into fat poodles, lapping cream in bourgeois drawing-rooms.

There is, as you may know, a mechanical problem in magazine editing. Stories and articles as a rule do not come out the right length; you have parts of pages blank, and as nature abhors a vacuum, there was evolved a type of composition known as " filler "—a certain number of verses with a simple rhyme pattern, dealing with flowers and sunsets and the polite aspects of sexual desire. But fifteen years ago there came a change; the highbrow

[135]

magazines took to giving whole pages to what was apparently meant as poetry, because it didn't go all the way to the right-hand margin, and every line began with a capital letter.   I used to read it in a state of wonderment —it must be supposed to have some quality, and what could that quality be?   It had no beauty of sound, no melody; on the contrary, it read like the baldest prose.   It had no depth of thought—it had seldom any thought whatever.   Here are lines taken from a presumable poem entitled " Attitude Under an Elm Tree," which appeared on the front page of the *Literary Review* of the *New York Evening Post*, one of the half-dozen great capitalist organs which determine what you and I and the rest of America shall consider culture.

> You were veiled at the jousting, you remember,
> Which enables me to imagine you without let or hin-
>   drance from the rigidness of fact;
> A condition not unproductive of charm if viewed
>   philosophically.
> Besides, your window gives upon a walled garden,
> Which I can by no means enter without dismounting
>   from my maple red charger,
> And this I will not do,
> Particularly as the garden belongs indubitably to your
>   ancestors.

Read that over several times—a score of times, as I have done.   Can you find one trace of beauty or charm?   Can you find one melodious or pleasing sound?   There was more to the poem, but the rest would not help you.   The " Attitude Under an Elm Tree " is merely the attitude of Amy Lowell standing on her head, because that was the only way she could get anyone to look at her.

How could such a phenomenon have come to be?   How could a woman with scant trace of singing gift, with very few thoughts of consequence to other human beings, have become the great lady-Cham of the world of tea-party poets, the founder of a school, or more accurately of a church, before whose altar the leisure-class choir bumped its forehead?   I have lived for the past twelve years in

[136]

the wilds of the West, where the only art-centre is Hollywood, so I do not attend the poetical tea-parties and gather the gossip of the *salons*.   It wasn't until I went to Boston, five years ago, to get material for " The Goose-step," that I came to realize who this lady-Cham of poetry was, and how her reputation had been made.   She was the sister of that able lawyer whom the Lee-Higginson banking interests have selected to convert Harvard University into a training school for strike-breakers; she was a Lowell, and I, in my naïve innocence, had failed to connect her poetical lucubrations with those famous lines which celebrate Boston as the land of the bean and the cod, where the Cabots speak only to Lowells, and the Lowells speak only to God.

Amy spoke to God, and He told her that since she was personally unbeautiful and stout, and partly crippled as result of an accident, she must find some other way of being distinguished than as a leader of the smart set.   He told her that to smoke big black cigars and swear volubly was not enough, because nowadays so many smart ladies are doing the same; the thing for Amy was to be a poet, and the founder of a cult.   Thus Amy's God, who had led her out of the house of bondage, and presented her with an income derived from the labour of some hundreds of mill-slaves in the town which bears her honoured name. And Amy, having centuries of pride and dominance behind her, set out to conquer a new world.   She had a huge mansion to live in, full of all the old books, and her mill-slaves enabled her to buy the new ones.   She sat herself down and practised for eight years, to see if it was possible for a woman with no trace of inspiration to fool all the critics and editors.   Her success is one more demonstration of the fact that if you have money and social prestige, you can get away with murder in America.

Reading her stuff in the magazines, I would find myself exclaiming, " This woman must live in a junk-shop! " Chinese vases and Japanese prints, Arabian shawls and Persian carpets, pearls from Ceylon and ivory from Africa

—all these things are the regulation stuff of poets, but
with Amy they become the whole of existence; her poetry
is a jumble of metaphors and allusions to articles of
merchandise. After she died, and her biographers and
friends conducted us into her home, we were able to understand; she had made the mansion into a curio-shop, full of
exotic wares, and these and her library and her garden
made up her world. It was an elaborate and expensive
garden, and comprised the whole of nature to this sick
and frustrated woman; supplying her with a thousand
images while she sat on summer days, lifting manfully at
her literary bookstraps. Alas, that the muse does not
recognize social position, nor even will-power and grit!
As Swinburne puts it:

> Yea, though we sang as angels in her ear,
> She would not hear!

The lady-Cham of New England letters travelled in state
and attended poetry conventions, and wrote critical articles,
assigning poetical rank to her social inferiors. Also she
distributed cheques subsidizing magazines, and invited
poets and editors to visit her. Poor devils of young writers,
trying to survive in our chaos of greed, would go away
singing gratitude, and editors would shiver with awe to
find themselves inside a Lowell mansion; so, year by
year, the bubble of Amy's reputation swelled. Since she
didn't have to put either rhyme or reason into what she
wrote, it was possible for her to turn out a vast quantity
of copy, and for years to monopolize the poetical output
of our highbrow magazines.

I submit this chapter to a friend who is on the " inside "
of the magazine world. He says, yes, there can be no
doubt that Amy Lowell bought her literary position. But
you have to know how to do it; her money was not
enough, it took also her mansion and her name. My
friend reminds me of an elderly gentleman by the name
of Frederick Fanning Ayer, who inherited a great fortune
and wanted to be known as a poet; he tried the method of

newspaper and magazine advertising, and spent a small fortune, and succeeded in selling only a few hundred copies of his book. You see, the poetry was too easy to understand, and also the money had come from sarsaparilla, which cannot be taken poetically. Says my cynical friend: " If that old gentleman had made his money out of good Scotch, and had known how to distribute a carload, he might easily have become the Amy Lowell of New York."

CHAPTER XXIX

THE HEART OF CHARITY

THE class struggle goes by contrasts; so, instead of proceeding to list the ivory tower poets of America, let me introduce you to a rebel poet, and show what a different welcome such a person receives from the critical machine.

Like Amy Lowell, this rebel was born with a golden spoon in her mouth; her father stood upon the utmost height possible to man in America, being president of the First National Bank of his home town. Everything that life can give to a woman—wealth, beauty, wit and social charm—the daughter possessed. But alas, the fates spoiled it by putting in too tender a heart; when she went into cities, and saw little children starving, she never had peace again. Instead of remaining a leader of fashion, she married a Socialist, and spent her possessions upon strike publicity. So she descended into the seven hells of poverty, pawning her jewels to the landlady, and sitting up all night doing hack literary work. She knew pain and fear, those twin hags that ride the backs of the workers.

In the days before she threw away her beauty, this woman had met a great poet, and he had fallen upon his knees before her. He was one of the aloof and haughty poets—at least in theory—and he told her about his aloof and haughty art. The woman, teasing him, called his muse an idle baggage, useless to mankind; the poets were pretenders, taking a pose of inspiration in order to impress the ladies they wooed; anybody could write poetry who was willing to take the trouble, " I could do it myself! " " Prove it," answered the poet, in a voice of scorn; and

[140]

the woman answered, " Tell me about some kind of poem, and I will write one." George Sterling, meaning to win this contest, showed the hardest of all kinds of poems, the sonnet; his pupil began practising, and presently she brought one to him, and he read it and wept. It was called " Love," and was hardly a fair test, because it was addressed to another man.[1]

The civilized world went to war. In Europe there were formed two lines of death, each nearly a thousand miles long, to which several thousand young men rushed each day to be turned into rotting corpses. Four years this continued; and never was there such a test of a woman poet. It is interesting to see what came from the leisure-class women, and then what came from the rebel women.

During the four years of the world war, Amy Lowell was the undisputed mistress of the poetical world of America; and you will find her reaction to the war in a volume, " Pictures of the Floating World," published in 1919. There are a total of one hundred and seventy-four poems in the book, and nine deal with the war. One tells about a landscape architect who went crazy and designed a garden like a fortress, and so lost his position and committed suicide. Another describes a camouflaged battleship, as seen from a ferry-boat in Boston Harbour. Another describes a fort; and so that you may know what great guns mean to a leisure-class lady, here are the eight lines of the climax of this art-work :

> Is it possible that, at night,
> The little flitter-bats
> Hang under the lever-wheels of the disappearing guns
> In their low emplacements
> To escape from the glare
> Of the search-lights,
> Shooting over the grasses
> To the sea?

---

[1] My friend Floyd Dell, whose advice in matters literary is usually excellent, tells me that I am barred from effective discussion of this woman poet by the fact of our relationship. Since I cannot change the relationship, I give the reader fair warning, and endeavour to subdue

During this same four-year period the rebel poet was entirely unknown to the critical world—as she is still. Her sonnets concerning the war appeared in obscure Socialist papers, and after the war twenty-five of them were published in a little pamphlet selling for twenty-five cents. It is an iron-clad rule of the leisure-class reviews that no book exists at less than a dollar and a half; cheaper books can't afford to advertise, and what are reviews for? Three dollars is a better advertising price, while a special numbered edition on hand-tooled Japanese paper bound in vellum at seven-fifty per copy is the seal of immortality. The " Sonnets of M. C. S." have been the solace of rebel workers in sweatshops and jails all over the world; but the haughty gentlemen of the capitalist critical machine do not know them. I have shown you what great guns mean to a lady-Brahmin of New England. Now let us see what they mean to a woman Socialist.

> The sharpened steel whips round, the black guns blaze.
>   Waste are the harvests, mute the songs of birds.
>   Out there in ice and mud the lowly herds
> Of peasant-folk in pitiful amaze
> Take their dire portion of the grief and want
>   Of this red cataclysm that has come
>   Upon the world. Colossal is the sum
> Of bodies in that field the buzzards haunt.
>
> So, all forgot is Reason's high estate!
>   Where Man once climbed and visioned Love and God
> He grovels now in primal Night. Aye, men
> Of mind are but as mindless brutes again :
>   The clod, through evolution, to the clod
> Has travelled back—to feed, to breed, to hate!

Amy Lowell had a garden. It was a great and costly garden, with rare plants from all over the world, a forest of trees to hide the poet from strangers, and hot-houses providing orchids and exotic blooms to stimulate her

myself to the rôle of reporter. For whatever errors of taste or judgment may be found in this chapter, I am to blame. I laboured for five years before I got my wife's consent to publish her sonnets; and I write this chapter without her consent—because I know that if I asked for it, I wouldn't get it!

imagination. This garden had been made by her ancestors, and her mill-slaves paid for the labour of many men to tend it. During the world war she entered this garden at night, and was unhappy, and she tells you about it on two pages of this same volume of " Pictures." First she lists the roses and the phlox and the heliotrope and the night-scented stocks and the folded poppies and the fireflies and the sweet alyssum and the snow-ball bush and the ladies' delight; then she reveals her grief, and we discover that it is not the red cataclysm that has come upon the world, but the thwarting of the dynastic impulses of Amy Lowell.

> Ah, Beloved, do you see those orange lilies?
> They knew my mother,
> But who belonging to me will they know
> When I am gone.

Also M. C. S. had a garden : made with her husband's help, as a respite from the labour of editing a Socialist magazine. She had planted cuttings got from the working-class neighbours, and tended them with her own hands, watering and working them in the hot sun of Southern California. Like Amy, the owner of this garden went into it at night, and failed to be completely happy—but for a somewhat different reason.

> I feel the terror in the world to-night—
>   Unbridled lust of power, and bridled lust
>   More cold but no less merciless. The dust
> Of perished legions drifts upon the bright
>   And tender winds of spring, a seal, blood-red,
> Upon man's last insanity. Surcease
> Of war? Ah, so they thought! To purchase peace
>   For aye, with their young blood! Ah, so they said!
>
> But peace is not upon the winds of spring.
>   The nostrils of new wars flare wide, and sniff
> The dust of heroes greedily, and fling
>   An evil breath upon the world—and if
> I chance to laugh because the spring is here,
> Pain stabs my heart and binds the wound with fear!

Search the books of the lady-Cham of New England, and amid all the lapidary work and bric-à-brac, the rugs and tapestries and mosaics, the furniture and jewels and ceramics, the carvings and ornaments and clocks, the sword-blades and poppy-seeds and fir-flower tablets, the yuccas confiding in passion-vines and the turkey buzzards chatting with the condors, the Indians climbing to the sky and the foxes trying to rape the moon—amid all this junk you will find here and there one human note, and that is when the poet admits that she is a lonely and beaten woman.   For example, in what she calls " A Fairy Tale," we hear a cry :

> Along the parching highroad of the world
> No other soul shall bear mine company.
> Always shall I be teased by semblances,
> With cruel impostures, which I trust awhile
> Then dash to pieces, as a careless boy
> Flings a kaleidoscope, which shattering
> Strews all the ground about with coloured sherds.

This is reasonably good poetry; and you will note that there is no obscurity about it, you don't have to puzzle over the meaning of a single word, nor to know anything about Japanese hokkus or fir-flower tablets of China.   Alongside it I set that sonnet by M. C. S. which caused George Sterling to weep; and again you will find that you don't have to rack your brains.   This poem bears the title " Love," and when it first appeared, in a Socialist magazine, Luther Burbank called it " the finest thing of the sort ever born of the human mind."

> You are so good, so bountiful, and kind;
>   You are the throb and sweep of music's wings;
> The heart of charity you are, and blind
>   To all my weaknesses; your presence brings
> The ointment and the myrrh to salve the thorn
>   Of daily fret of concourse.   That you live
> Is like to bugles trumping judgment-morn,
> And stranger than the cry the new-born give.
>
> And yet. some day you will go hence.   And I
>   Shall wander lonely here awhile, and then—
> Then I, like you, shall lay me down and die.
>   Oh, sweetheart, kiss me, kiss me once again!
> Oh, kiss me many times, and hold me near:
>   For what of us, when we no more are here?

CHAPTER XXX

CHOOSE YOUR POET

DURING the days when I was a hungry hack-writer, there appeared in a New York newspaper a letter making known to lovers of literature that a man who had revealed gifts as a poet was earning his living digging the New York subway. The name of the poet was not given, but I learned later that it was Edwin Arlington Robinson; and presumably some help must have been found, for the subway labourer devoted himself to writing, and has just published a long narrative which I see advertised as " the greatest poem that has yet been written in America." A part of it was read in a theatre in New York, and a great audience showed tremendous delight. Do I need to tell you that this masterpiece does not deal with the digging of subways, nor with any other aspect of American wage-slavery? No, it is called " Tristram," and its theme is a domestic triangle in a royal family dead some half-dozen centuries.

Here and there I have found some pleasure in Mr. Robinson's books: for example, his " Miniver Cheevy, child of scorn," who " cursed the commonplace " and " missed the mediæval grace of iron clothing." That is a sample of the acid with which this poet does his etching. You note that it is an individual foible he deals with; and it is always thus. He is, apparently, entirely lacking in a social sense. His experience in the subway trenches taught him nothing. He had no feeling of kinship with his fellow-toilers; all he wanted was to make his escape from the slave-world, and live comfortably at the MacDowell Colony, and become a dignified poet of old-fashioned American individualism. As one of his adorers puts it, very haughtily, " Mr. Robinson does not wish to preach anything. He does not consider the world as in the immediate path of salvation."

And so, as the years go by, we see happening to him what happens to all gentlemen poets—his writing comes to possess what the critics praise as " subtlety." Having nothing really important to say, and no deep creative impulse, the poet concentrates more and more upon his manner of saying things; he racks his mind to devise intricate and complicated and involved modes of utterance.

I used to be fooled by that. When I was a youth I read every word of Robert Browning, patiently consulting footnotes, looking up names in encyclopædias, digging out learned papers of the Browning Society to find out what " Sordello " is about. But now that I am as old as Browning, I know that he did not have many original or profound ideas; he was a Victorian gentleman of travel and odd learning, who liked to wrap up obvious and commonplace statements in mystifying language; filling his poetry with references to forgotten persons and things, of as much consequence to you and me as the addresses of all the Smiths in the telephone directory of Kalamazoo, Michigan.

I take up a recent volume by Mr. Robinson, " The Man Who Died Twice." It tells the story of a musician who wrecks his art by dissipation. I open the volume at random, and find myself reading about music

> Blown down by choral horns out of a star
> To quench those drums of death with singing fire
> Unfelt by man before.

Of course I recognize the right of a poet straining after an effect to mix his metaphors now and then. I remember that Hamlet spoke of taking arms against a sea of trouble. But if Hamlet had talked about blowing

music out of a star to quench drums of death with fire
that sang and had never been felt before—I would surely
have said that he ought to have stopped and got clear in
his mind what he was trying to convey to mine.

And now the new book, " Tristram." I debate
whether out of a sense of loyalty to my job I am going
to wade through two hundred pages about the sexual
entanglements of Isolt of Ireland and Isolt of the White
Hands, away back in the days of Malory and the Knights
of the Round Table. I pick up the volume and trace
a long, involved paragraph, in which Mr. Robinson says
the same obvious thing three times over, and each time
in a more complicated and fantastic fashion—until in the
end he gets lost in his labyrinth of words, and forgets to
finish his sentence! So I forget to finish this " greatest
poem that has yet been written in America."

Instead, I tell you about an American university teacher,
a friend of mine and teacher of my son. He dreamed
the dream that there might be justice in America, that
men might no longer commit mass murder, and rob
others of the fruits of toil. A wild and dangerous dream,
and a young professor of English who thus steps out
of his specialty will be unpopular with his dean, and
also with his wife's relatives. This friend of mine was
trying to be a poet, and he married a young girl, and
presently made the discovery that the seeds of hereditary
insanity were developing in her mind. So with enemies
at home and abroad, he had a painful time, and when
his wife drank poison he nearly lost his own mind;
indeed, some think he did—his hair turned white, and
his face became haggard, and the students, when they
pass him, tap their foreheads and say, " There's a nut! "
Just so they said about Dante long ago, and about
John Bunyan, and William Blake, and a hundred
others who have extended the boundaries of the soul's
experience.

And now, which would you rather read about: Isolt
of the White Hands, who pined away because her

husband loved another woman, or William Ellery Leonard, Professor of English at the University of Wisconsin?   How romantic the first sounds, and how commonplace the second—a scandal item in to-morrow morning's newspaper!   If you read the book of sonnets in which the professor has exposed his tortured soul, you may be further disconcerted, because you won't find mixed metaphors, nor obscure references to be looked up, nor intricacies to be disentangled.   What you will find is a story so tragic and terrible, told with a drive so compelling, and with beauty so tender, and wisdom so deep, and pity so all-embracing—I won't say that " Two Lives " is the greatest poem that has yet been written in America, because I remember Emerson's " Threnody," and Poe's " Israfel," and Whitman's " Drum Taps," and Sterling's " Duandon," and a number of others that I shall name; but I will say that it is what I mean by great poetry, dealing with everyday realities of the America we live in, and dealing with them from a point of view which embraces the future as well as the past, and is free and creative in the highest sense of those words.

CHAPTER XXXI

THE FAMILY LAWYER

I HAVE got this far in my manuscript, when a telegram interrupts my labours. The bookstores of Boston have removed my novel, " Oil! " from sale, at the instigation of a church censorship. You remember I wrote, a little way back, that when you get a censor you generally get a fool, and sometimes also a knave. So now we shall see!

It was my intention in " Money Writes! " to be judicious, and leave out my own writings. But when you are in a war, you cannot always choose the battlefield; in this case the police department of Boston has made the choice, and so I state that " Oil! " is a novel portraying America's most speculative and spectacular industry, and incidentally picturing the moral and political breakdown of our ruling classes. The censors will pretend to be shocked by half a dozen brief glimpses of Hollywood petting-parties; but what they really want is to shut off a book of revolutionary criticism.

The Boston *Herald* telegraphs asking what I mean to do; and I answer that I will come and sell the book myself. But meantime the authorities proceed to arrest a twenty-year-old bookseller's clerk and rush him to trial. So here I am on a transcontinental train, on my way to appear as witness for Mr. John Gritz of the Smith and McCance bookstore, in that city of the bean and the cod where Amy Lowell spoke to God, and where Amy Lowell's brother has just been appointed upon a commission to decide the fate of Sacco and Vanzetti.

The officials of the Union Pacific Railroad find me out, and give me a taste of Mencken's adventures. The

passenger agent at Salt Lake City appears with an automobile and whisks me off to see the great Mormon
Temple in twenty-five minutes, and hear the greatest
organ in the world play " Annie Laurie "! The
Mormon brethren load me up with their propaganda;
and now I sit, gazing out at red mountains and fields
of young sugar-beets, and reading over again the wonder-
story of how a farmer's boy in New York state dug up
the golden tablets, Urim and Thummin, and how God
sent the angel Moroni to deliver a new gospel, the Book
of Mormon. You may doubt the tale, but I have just
seen the angel, shining on the top of his temple, twelve
feet five and one-half inches high, and made of hammered
copper covered with gold leaf.

In all the world it would not be possible to find more
naïve nonsense than the Mormon mythology; and yet
these people have huge granite buildings, and a beautiful
city with wide avenues—apparently the angel Moroni
revealed the automobile to old Brigham Young. They
have several hundred thousand faithful and devoted
workers, and control the sugar trust and the copper trust
and a large section of the Republican party. I sit and
ponder the problem—which is better, to have faith in
naïve nonsense and build a civilization; or to have no
faith whatever, and see your civilization crumbling under
your feet?

Which brings us to our next poet, Edgar Lee Masters.
Some years ago he published a book of free verse called
" The Spoon River Anthology," and all literary America
read it and shivered. " Spoon River " is an imaginary
village of the Middle West—we may guess that it lies not
very far from Petersburg, Illinois, in which Mr. Masters
grew up. He imagines a graveyard, with head-stones
containing epitaphs of an unprecedented sort, telling the
truth about the wretches that lie beneath: everything
unpleasant in human nature—envy, hatred, malice and
all uncharitableness, plus a few feeble gleams of aspiration, inevitably brought to quick extinction. Mr. Masters

bears a heavy grudge against his fellow-beings, and a still heavier one against the fate which has created them; he is as ingenious as Maupassant in devising situations to expose the irony of mortal hopes.

And then a series of novels, which, like all other novels, are propaganda for a certain point of view. These of Masters exhibit a leisure class, wandering about lost in the midst of luxury, having no idea what use to make of it. Their author once wrote me that I was mistaken in thinking that he did not realize the dominance of economic forces over his people. So perhaps I had better not pass judgment, but simply say that " Mirage " and " The Nuptial Flight " are powerful social documents, which have had very little of the critical attention they deserve.

Imagine them being written by an old family lawyer, who sits in his private office and has a string of men and women come before him, revealing the inmost secrets of their lives; all the base things they have done or hope yet to do, their cowardly fears and ravenous greeds. It must be a trying kind of life, and judging from the books of Edgar Lee Masters, the only faith it left him is in Stephen A. Douglas and the pro-slavery Democrats of seventy years ago. His heart warms to the " little giant," I think because the reformers fought him.

One other theme moves him to tenderness, and that is boys and the life of boys. But they must be boys of a long time ago, who can be seen through a haze of romance—boys who were simple and natural and jolly, and never had to be reformed with a birch-rod or a trunk-strap! But alas, even these ideal boys grow up, and make a lot of money, and drink cocktails and play with their friends' wives; and what is to be done about it is something concerning which the Chicago ex-lawyer has had no angel Moroni to descend from heaven and tell him —and so the readers of these books will not be led to build granite temples and make the desert blossom with sugar-beets!

CHAPTER XXXII

ADONAIS

I COME now to the dearest friend I ever had among men. Since he is gone, there seems a large hole in the world.

It was Jack London who gave him to me, some twenty-five years ago, sending me a book of poems, " The Testimony of the Suns," by George Sterling. In the fly-leaf he wrote, " I have a friend, the dearest in this world." Since friendship is a thing without limits, I also took possession of this poet. We corresponded for seven or eight years, and then I went to California to visit him, and stayed several months at Carmel. A year or two later the fates played a strange prank upon us— he lost his heart to the woman who was later to become my wife.

How much of that strange story will it be decent for me to tell? It is hard for me to judge, because what the world calls " tact " is not my strong point; and I cannot ask my wife, because she is ill, and since our friend's dreadful death, I do not mention him. Some day the story will be known, because he wrote her a hundred or so of sonnets, the most beautiful in the world. For sixteen years his attitude never changed : her marriage made no difference—when he came to visit us, he would follow her about with his eyes, and sit and murmur her name as if under a spell; our friends would look at us and smile, but George never cared what anyone thought. All his life long women had flung themselves at his head, and he had given them the pity and sympathy his gentle nature could not withhold. It was the tragedy of his fate that the woman he respected was the one he failed to win. When first he met her, he wrote, in a copy of

" The House of Orchids," " I have thought of this as my last book.   Do you wish it to be the last? "   But later he wrote, " To know that you live is enough.   You have given me back my art."

When he first met her, and was bringing her a sonnet every day, they were walking on Riverside Drive in New York, and I chanced to come along.   She was working on a book, and I, with my customary reformer's impulse, remarked, " You have been overworking; you are worn out."   She answered, " This poet has just been telling me that I look like a star in alabaster." . " Well, I think you look like a skull," I said, and went on, leaving the poet grinding his teeth in fury.   " Some day I am going to kill that man! " he exclaimed; and his companion replied, " That is the first man that ever told me the truth in my life.   I am going to marry him! "

So she did; and for a while there appeared a certain element of acerbity in the criticisms which George would pen upon the margins of my manuscripts.   But tenderness and patience were the least contribution I could make to our friendship; so I would laugh, and presently George would grow remorseful, and tell me that maybe I was half right after all.

There were two men in him, and a strange duel for ever going on in his soul.   In his literary youth he had fallen under the spell of Ambrose Bierce, an able writer, a bitter black cynic, and a cruel, domineering old bigot. He stamped inerasably upon George's sensitive mind the heartless art-for-art's-sake formula, the notion of a poet as a superior being, aloof from the problems of men, and writing for the chosen few.   On the other hand, George was a chum of Jack London and others of the young " reds," and became a Socialist and remained one to the end.   Bierce quarrelled with him on this account, and broke with him, as he did with everyone else.   But in art the Bierce influence remained dominant, and George Sterling would write about the interstellar spaces and the writhing of oily waters in San Francisco harbour, and

[153]

the white crests of the surf on Point Lobos, and the loves of ancient immoral queens.

After which he would go about the streets of New York on a winter night, and come back without his overcoat, because he had given it to some poor wretch on the bread-line; he would be shivering, not with cold, but with horror and grief, and would break all the art-for-art's-sake rules, and pour out some lines of passionate indignation, which he refused to consider poetry, but which I assured him would outlive his fancy stuff.

At the time of our " mourning pickets " on Broadway, during the Colorado coal strike of 1914, George was in New York, and his " star in alabaster " was walking up and down eight hours a day amid a mob of staring idlers, her husband in jail and only a few " wobblies " and Jewish " reds " from the East Side to keep her company. George appeared and offered her his arm. " Go away," she said; " this is no job for a poet! " But of course he would not go; he stuck by her side for two weeks, and up at the Lambs' Club, where he was staying, the art-snobs and wealthy loafers " joshed " him mercilessly—some even insulted him, and there was a fight or two. During these excitements George wandered down to the Battery, and looking out over the bay he wrote that stunning poem, " To the Goddess of Liberty " :

> Oh! is it bale-fire in thy brazen hand—
> The traitor-light set on betraying coasts
> To lure to doom the mariner? . . .

You will find that in my anthology, " The Cry for Justice." Also his song about Babylon, which really is New York, and San Francisco too :

> In Babylon, high Babylon,
>   What gear is bought and sold?
> All merchandise beneath the sun
>   That bartered is for gold;
> Amber and oils from far beyond
>   The desert and the fen,
> And wines whereof our throats are fond—
>   Yea! and the souls of men!

In Babylon, grey Babylon,
  What goods are sold and bought?
Vesture of linen subtly spun,
  And cups from agate wrought;
Raiment of many-coloured silk
  For some fair denizen,
And ivory more white than milk—
  Yea! and the souls of men! . . .

Also I mention his tribute to the Episcopal Church—
and others—quoted in " The Profits of Religion "—

Within the House of Mammon his priesthood stands alert
By mysteries attended, by dusk and splendours girt,
Knowing, for faiths departed, his own shall still endure,
And they be found his chosen, untroubled, solemn, sure.

Within the House of Mammon the golden altar lifts
Where dragon-lamps are shrouded as costly incense drifts—
A dust of old ideals, now fragrant from the coals,
To tell of hopes long-ended, to tell the death of souls.

I have told how my friend Mencken asked me to
write about Sterling without mentioning alcohol.   The
first time I visited George I was to be the orator at a
dinner of the Ruskin Club in Oakland, and George was
to read a poem.   We met at the Bohemian Club in
San Francisco, and George drank a couple of cocktails on
an empty stomach, and we set out.   On the ferry-boat I
had difficulty in understanding his conversation; and
finally the painful realization dawned over me that the
great poet was drunk.   My own father had been a
drinking man, and several of my relatives in the South,
so I was no stranger to the spectacle; but this was the
first time I had ever seen an intellectual man in that
condition; and the next day I wrote George a note, saying
it was too painful, and I was not going to stay at Carmel.
He came running over to my house, and with tears in
his eyes vowed that he would never touch another drop
while I was in California.   Sometimes I have wished I
might have stayed the rest of my life; it might be that is
the greatest service I could have rendered to the future.
From that day on I never saw George with any sign of

drink on him. He visited us at Croton, and went over the huge manuscript of " The Cry for Justice," and chopped down some dead chestnut trees and cut them up for our fireplace. He was an athlete, and beautiful to look at— a face like Dante's, grave and yet tender, and a tall, active body. We have a snapshot of him in bathing-trunks, standing upon the rocks of Point Lobos with an abalone hook in his hand, and nothing more graceful was ever planned by a Greek sculptor.

George went back to San Francisco and lived at the Bohemian Club, where some admirer had bequeathed him a room for life. It is a place of satyrs, and the worst environment that could have been imagined under the circumstances. George had begun his drinking with Jack London and Ambrose Bierce, and then it was all gaiety and youth, the chanting of George's " Abalone Song," and the " grove play," and the Bohemian " jinks." But later on in life it becomes something different. Others may sing the romance and the charm of San Francisco; to me it is a plague-city, where all the lovely spirits drink poison—first Nora May French, and then Carrie Sterling, and then Jack London, and then my best of friends.

George had more admirers than any other man I ever knew, and he gave himself to them without limit. When they were drinking, he could not sit apart; and so tragedy closed upon him. He would come to visit us in Pasadena, and always then he was " on the wagon," and never going to drink again; but we could see his loneliness and his despair—not about himself, for he was too proud to voice that, but for mankind, and for the universe. It may seem a strange statement, that a poet could be killed by the nebular hypothesis; but M. C. S. declares that is what happened to George Sterling. I believe the leaders of science now reject the nebular hypothesis, and have a new one; but meantime, they had fixed firmly in George's mind the idea that the universe is running down like a clock, that in some millions of years the earth will be cold, and in some hundreds of millions of years the sun will be cold, and so what difference does it make what we poor insects do? You will find that at the beginning, in " The Testimony of the Suns," and at the end in the drama, " Truth." It is what one might call applied atheism.

Once, M. C. S. tells me, George offered never to drink again, if she would ask him not to. But her notion of fair play did not permit her to do this. What could she give him in return? The cares of her own life were too many; she had a husband who refused to be afraid of his enemies, and so she had to be afraid for two, and there were long periods when she could not even answer George's letters. He stayed in San Francisco, and now and then he would say he was coming to see us, and when he did not come, we would know why.

Mencken was coming to visit George, and just before his coming George was drunk. He was fifty-six years old, and there was no longer any fun about it, but an agony of pain and humiliation; and so he took cyanide of potassium, as he had many times threatened to do. To me it is something so cruel that I would not talk about it, were it not for the next generation of poets and writers, who are parroting the art-for-art's-sake devilment, and dancing to hell with John Bootleg.

Consider my friend Mencken. The death of this beautiful and noble and generous-souled poet has taught him nothing whatsoever; he writes the same cheerfully flippant letters in celebration of the American saloon. " Whatever George told you in moments of katzenjammer, I am sure that he got a great deal more fun out of alcohol than woe. It was his best friend for many years and made life tolerable. He committed suicide in the end, not because he wanted to get rid of drink, but simply because he could no longer drink enough to give him any pleasure."

Was more poisonous nonsense ever penned by an intellectual man? How many pleasures there are which do not pall with age, and do not destroy their devotees! The pleasures of knowledge, for example—of gaining it,

[157]

and helping to spread it. The pleasure of sport; I play tennis, and it is just as much fun to me at forty-eight as it was at fourteen. The pleasures of music; I play the violin, after a fashion, and my friend Mencken plays it better, I hope—and does he find that every year he has to play more violently in order to hear it, and that after playing he suffers agonies of sickness, remorse and dread? I say for shame upon an intellectual man who cannot make such distinctions; for shame upon a teacher of youth who has no care whether he sets their feet upon the road to wisdom and happiness, or to misery and suicide!

Let George Sterling speak from his grave the last words upon the subject—a few lines from " The Man I Might Have Been."

> Clear-visioned with betraying night,
>   I count his merits o'er,
> And get no comfort from the sight,
>   Nor any cure therefor.
> I'd mourn my desecrated years
>   (His maimed and sorry twin),
> But well he knows my makeshift tears—
>   The man I might have been.
>
> Decisively his looks declare
>   The heart's divine success;
> He held no parley with despair,
>   Nor pact with wantonness. . . .
> O Fates that held us at your choice,
>   How strange a web ye spin!
> Why chose ye not with equal voice
>   The man I might have been?

CHAPTER XXXIII

BACCHUS' TRAIN

Is alcohol ever to be credited with the flights of genius? I asked this question of George Sterling, saying that I wanted to quote him as an authority. He answered, instantly, "Never! Absolutely never! You write things that you think are marvellous, but next morning when you read them over, you discover they are nonsense."

The opposite belief was held by a near-genius whose memory has been piously embalmed by his wife, in a beautiful book called " The Road to the Temple." I hope I shall not pain her too much if I say that the excellence of the book seems to me far more the product of Susan Glaspell than of George Cram Cook. Susan is in her own right a dramatist of power; while " Jig," as his friends called him, was a poet only to his devoted wife. She gives us pages upon pages of his free verse, and it seems to me an easy kind of poetry to write.

Many years ago Jig Cook wrote a novel, " The Chasm," and it made me happy because it was an out-and-out Socialist novel, and I pray day and night for American Socialist novels. In twenty-four years I have had only two answers—the other one being " Comrade Yetta." So I had every prejudice in favour of Comrade Cook, and also of his wife, who has given me an almost Socialist drama, " Inheritors." When I read that Jig had gone to Greece to become a shepherd, I set it down as a war-casualty; but now I read between the lines of his widow's pious tribute, and realize that Jig had cast in his poetical fortunes with

[159]

Bacchus, and prohibition had made these rites too expensive in America.

Let Susan tell you about it in her own way:

" All his life this man had a habit of occasionally getting drunk and seeing truth from a new place. He was far from ashamed of this. He valued it in himself. He saw then, saw what was pretending, in himself, in others. It would begin in good times with friends—self-consciousness and timidities going down in the warmth of sympathetic drinking. There was a sublimated playfulness, ideas became a great game, and in play with them something that had not been before came into being."

And then again, she quotes her husband:

" ' You see, they drank only with their bellies. But true drinking is an affair of the head and heart. There must be a second, finer ferment in the mind—a brewing and refining of raw wit and wisdom.' Long afterwards, on Parnassos, he had what I venture to call a somewhat godlike relation of wine and vision. Drinking was one of the things in which Jig succeeded, in which he realized himself as human being and artist. Yet he saw the black thing it may become."

Yes, he saw it; but apparently his wife saw it only dimly. He was full of dreams of classic glory, and yearned to Greece, as a child seeking the pot of gold at the foot of the rainbow. His wife followed him dutifully; and they saw Parnassos, the hope of his life, and then " suddenly, very tired by the deep excitements, ' Well, come on, let's go some place and get a drink.' " They went to many places and had many drinks, and Susan writes as follows:

" Next day was one of those times of a particular beauty in our household. ' Hang-over days ' we called them, and they have a subtle, fragile, sensitive quality. Satisfied by a violent encounter with life, one has a rarefied sense of being something nearer pure spirit. They are isolated days, no use trying to go on with things. Perhaps not so isolated as suspended. A woman who has never lived with

a man who sometimes ' drinks to excess ' has missed one
of the satisfactions that is like a gift—taking care of the
man she loves when he has this sweetness as of a newborn
soul."

I will make my comment on this as brief as possible; I
cannot recall ever having read a greater piece of nonsense
from the pen of a modern emancipated woman. The plain
truth, which stares at us between every line of the closing
narrative, is that poor Jig Cook, a poet who pinned his
faith to Bacchus instead of to Minerva, was at the age of
fifty a pitiful white-haired sot, dead to the Socialist movement, dead to the whole modern world, wandering about
lost among dirty and degraded peasants. He died of an
infection utterly mysterious to his wife—who apparently
knows nothing of the effects of alcohol in destroying the
cells of the liver and breaking down the natural immunity
of the body.

Why write these cruel words? The poor fellow paid
for his blunders, and he is gone. But I look about me,
and how many of our young men of genius I see dancing
in this satyr train! I have named the ones who are dead
—O. Henry and Stephen Crane and Ambrose Bierce and
Jack London and George Sterling; but what shall I say
about the ones who are on the way to death?

I meet an intimate friend of one of our most brilliant
young dramatists. " How is he? " I ask, full of friendly
hopes; and the answer is that he goes off on drinking bouts
that last two or three weeks, and his friends never know
if they will be able to pull him through. I meet an old-
time journalist who has an absorbingly interesting story
of real life, and I say, " You ought to get So-and-so to help
you make that into a best-seller." So-and-so is one of our
most brilliant young novelists; and the answer of the
journalist is, " No, thank you! He is doing his writing
on booze. He gets drunk in public and makes violent
rows, and I'm too good a quarreller myself." In conversation with another friend I refer to a most eminent of our
respectable poets. " That old gentleman who soaks him-

L

self in gin," remarks my friend—" how does he ever find time to write? "

Shall I go on? George Sterling wrote me that he had had a visit from one of our most brilliant satiric poets; and I asked, " How did you find him? " The answer was, " If he was interested in anything but booze and women, I couldn't discover it." I learn that a relative of mine knows a bright young novelist of the fashionable set, and I ask, " What sort of a person is he? " The answer comes, " He and his wife are both drinking themselves to death." I receive an abusive letter from a successful novelist, who has risen from the workers, and whom I once helped; now he is furious with me because, forsooth, I have dared to give help to a rival young writer. I ask a mutual friend what that can mean, and the answer is, " Oh, he's boozing, that's all."

All my life I have lived in the presence of fine and beautiful men going to their death because of alcohol. I call it the greatest trap that life has set for the feet of genius; and I record my opinion, that the prohibition amendment is the greatest step in progress taken by America since the freeing of the slaves. That *obiter dictum* is dedicated to my friend Mencken, " to make him yell."

CHAPTER XXXIV

THE EX-FURNACEMAN

TWENTY years ago I had what the New York newspapers were pleased to call a " Socialist colony "; and one day there turned up at this place a run-away student from Yale University. Harry Sinclair Lewis was his name, and we called him " Hal "; he was tall and lanky, red-headed and talkative, merry, and as we learned later, observant. He applied for the job of tending our furnace without knowing anything about it; and as none of us knew any more than he, we let him. He sat round our four-sided fireplace in the evenings and got a complete education in every aspect of the radical movement, which was far more useful to him than anything he could have got at Yale.

Now he is the most famous of American novelists, and I shine in his reflected glory. About fifty per cent. of the strangers I meet tell me how much they enjoyed " Main Street "; or else they frown, and I know they are blaming me for " Elmer Gantry." Even newspapers do it; the editor of a religious paper has just damned me for having challenged God in a Kansas City church. I am getting uneasy for fear the recording angel may have got it wrong in his records, and what will I do if I wake up in hell?

My ex-furnaceman's books are so well known that I won't take the time to tell about them, but will come at once to my point, which is that he does not make as much use of his radical education as the good of his country requires. He knows the movement, and it motivates his criticism; but some day I hope that he won't

feel he has to camouflage his knowledge so carefully. In
" Main Street " there is a " wobbly," but we are elaborately kept from knowing that he is anything so dreadful.
That was all right, because Hal was a young publisher's
reader who had made a little money writing for Colonel
Lorimer, and taken a year off in an effort to win his
freedom. But now that he is the most famous novelist
in America, and close to a millionaire, surely he might
venture to tell the whole truth!

I take the case of " Arrowsmith," concerning which I
have facts to contribute. There is a character in this fine
novel by the name of Max Gottlieb, represented as being
a master scientific researcher. It bears resemblance to
Jacques Loeb, so much so that everyone takes it to be
Loeb. But it isn't; and it so happens that I knew Loeb
intimately, and can say exactly what Lewis did to Loeb
to turn him into Gottlieb.

The most conspicuous fact about Loeb was that he was
a thoroughly trained and ardent Social-democrat of the
old German type. He never—at least not until the war
—made the slightest concealment of his revolutionary
beliefs. But that was an aspect of Loeb which would not
have endeared him to the American novel-reading public;
and so what did Lewis do? He performed a major
surgical operation, and cut out Loeb's Socialism, and threw
it into the garbage-can. And what did he put into its
place? Why, Max Gottlieb gets drunk. A great scientist
may not revolt against capitalism, but it is quite respectable for him to revolt against prohibition!

" Arrowsmith " comes down to the post-war period;
and so I mention another aspect of Jacques Loeb—a great
scientist from Germany brow-beaten, cowed, literally dying
of humiliation at the treatment he has received from
American public opinion. In 1922, when I made a tour of
America to gather material for " The Goose-step," I visited
Loeb at Wood's Hole, and he poured out his heart to me;
telling the story of the time-serving and Mammon-worship
he had seen during twenty years of American academic

life, first at the University of Chicago and then at the
University of California. I made copious notes under
Loeb's eyes; but no sooner was I gone than fear seized
him, and he wrote me the most abject and pitiful letters
—do not for God's sake mention his name, do not write
anything that could be identified as having come from
him, for fear of ruining his research work. Will anyone
say that is not drama? Will anyone say that such a Max
Gottlieb could not have been made interesting in a novel?

I wrote to Sinclair Lewis, protesting against the lack of
social understanding on the part of this character and
others. I have a right to do this, because I have been
his friend for twenty years, and he has acknowledged me
as one of his teachers. I had heard that he was going to
write a " preacher novel," and I begged him not to repeat
this—shall I say evasion?—in his new book. I pointed
out that however ignorant a bacteriologist may be, it is
impossible for a Methodist clergyman in America not to
have some information on social questions; because Harry
F. Ward has an organization for the purpose of seeing
that they get appealed to and informed. In order to make
certain that my friend knew what the Methodist clergy
are getting, I sent him a copy of the four-page semi-
monthly paper, the *Social Service Bulletin*, published by
the Methodist Federation for Social Service in New York
City.

And what came of it? You have read " Elmer
Gantry," and you know that nothing came of it. Elmer
knows nothing and hears nothing about social justice, and
neither do any of the other clerical persons in the book.
Instead, Elmer Gantry, the villain, does like the scientific
heroes—he gets drunk. I do not mean to assert there
are not Methodist and Baptist clergymen who get drunk,
and carry on intrigues with the married ladies of their
congregation; but will anyone seriously maintain that the
problem of the clergy who so behave is anything like so
general or so urgent as the problem of the clergy who have
rich parishioners, and do not speak out against wage-

slavery and political corruption for fear of what these parishioners may think and say and do?

It is an awkward matter for me to criticize " Elmer Gantry," when I have a rival novel on the market, and am being beaten in the sales. But let me record that when I read " Babbitt," I emitted a whoop of delight, and that whoop was widely advertised by the publishers. Nothing would please me more than to whoop again—but it won't be for a novel which jeers at the Protestant Churches of America because they put the prohibition laws on the statute books, and are going to stick to the job until they get the laws enforced.

My friend Hal has promised me to write a labour novel; and that is what I beg for. I do not ask a work of propaganda, but a work of facts that will introduce the American people to this unknown world. Let the novelist show bureaucracy and graft in the old-line unions— nothing needs more to be done. Let him show the weaknesses of the radical movement, its miserable factional wrangling, its dogmatism and narrowness—I have been pleading against these errors, and I am ready to " stand the gaff." But let the novelist also make clear—he knows it as well as I know it—that our society is in agony from the poisoning of the profit motive; and let him portray the new forces that are germinating among the organized workers and farmers, to put an end to the poisoning. If he will write this, he will displease a million or two of his readers, and perhaps lose them for a time; but he will perform for the American people the greatest literary service in their history.

CHAPTER XXXV

THE SPRINGS OF PESSIMISM

ONE great service was rendered to American literature by George Cram Cook. He founded the Provincetown Theatre, and discovered Eugene O'Neill: a wild boy who had run away from home, and shipped as a sailor, and lived a vagabond life in various ports of the world. He happened to be in Provincetown " with a trunkful of plays," when the little group of radicals were trying to start a proletarian drama. So he got a hearing, which the commercial theatre of Broadway would not have given him in a thousand years. And so the commercial theatre of Broadway has been mocked.

If you think that my understanding of proletarian art is Socialist lectures disguised as novels and soap-box orations preached from a stage, then let me hasten to say that these early plays of O'Neill are part of what I want and have got. Here is a man who writes about the sea, from the point of view of the wage-slaves of the sea, with full knowledge, insight, and pity; yet, so far as I can recall, there is not one word of direct propaganda, hardly even of indirect. Let a man show capitalism as it really is in any smallest corner—as O'Neill has done in " Bound East for Cardiff "—and the message of revolt rings from every sentence.

And then " The Emperor Jones ": the first O'Neill play to reach California, and so the first that I saw on the stage. A rigid Leninist would call that a reactionary play, because it suggests a permanent, hereditary inferiority

of the black race. But it is a play so full of pity and
terror, of truly magical entrance into the heart of savage
humanity, that it operates to humble pride and break
down barriers. I have put so much denunciation into
this book, you may think me hard to please; so take
note that I am ready to praise what I can, and not afraid
to hail a masterpiece in my own day. " The Emperor
Jones " is my idea of great drama and great poetry, a
leap of the imagination and an enlargement of the
possibilities of the theatre.

And then " The Hairy Ape," which my friend Floyd
Dell hailed as definitely reactionary. For my part, I am
glad of small favours; I note a short scene in a headquarters of the I.W.W., in which these men behave
exactly as they would have done in reality. Am I
correct in saying that it is the first and only time this
has happened in the acted theatre of America? If O'Neill
had chosen one of these rebel workers for his hero, I
would have been still more pleased, but the theatre public
would have waited some years to hear of it. As the
author of " Singing Jailbirds," I do not speak at a guess!

Our great proletarian playwright has grown pessimistic, and is now groping in the fogs of metaphysics.
I followed him for an uncomfortable evening in " The
Great God Brown," and when he was through I didn't
know what he was driving at, and neither did he—I
know it, because he was indiscreet enough to write a
long statement on the programme, trying to tell me. My
counter-statement will be briefer, and nobody will have
any doubt what I mean.

Pessimism is mental disease. It is that wherever and
under whatever circumstances it appears, in art and
philosophy, as in everyday life. It means illness in the
person who voices it, and in the society which produces
that person. If it continues unchecked in an individual,
it is a symptom of his moral breakdown; if it prevails
in the literature, art, drama, politics, or philosophy of a
nation it means that nation is in course of decay.

All truly great art is optimistic. The individual artist is happy in his creative work, and in its reception by his public; the public is active and sound, occupied in mastering life and expanding the social forces. It is only when those forces exhaust themselves, that the art public enjoys contemplating moral impotence, and that the individual artist does not know whether life is worth living.

The fact that practically all great art is tragic does not in any way change the above thesis. I have named the three great classic dramas, the " Prometheus Bound " of Æschylus, the " Prometheus Unbound " of Shelley, and the " Samson Agonistes " of Milton. All three are tragic; but in each case the hero struggles in the cause of a new faith. And the same thing applies to " The Emperor Jones," and " The Hairy Ape "; their individual protagonists go down to defeat, but they struggle for light, and this impulse is communicated to us.

Capitalist art, when produced by artists of sincerity and intelligence, is pessimistic, because capitalism is dying; it has no morals, and can have none, being the negation of morality in social affairs. Proletarian art is optimistic, because it is only by hope that the workers can act, or dream of acting. Proletarian art has a morality of brotherhood and service, because it is only by these qualities that the masses can achieve their freedom.

And in order to avoid cheap sneers and misunderstandings, let me add that there is a capitalist art of false optimism, based upon the master-class desire to keep the worker in ignorance as to their conditions and prospects. To unmask this art is the first task of the social rebel, and I have tried to do my share of this service.

CHAPTER XXXVI

A VISIT TO BOSTON

Two or three years ago it happened that a Russian-Jewish family, residing in Boston, sought to Americanize itself by changing its name from Kabotski to Cabot. This occasioned distress to the family which for three centuries had been speaking only to the Lowells, and they sought by court action to compel the interlopers to adopt some other name. Their efforts failed; and some wag composed a new version of the old jingle:

> Here's to the city of Boston,
>   The land of the bean and the cod,
> Where the Lowells speak only to Cabots,
>   And the Cabots speak Yiddish, by God.

Now, having alighted from my transcontinental train, and spent two weeks in the venerable city, I submit a third version, as follows:

> Here's to the city of Boston,
>   The land of the bean and the cod,
> Where the Lowells won't let you buy " Oil! "
>   And you send to New York, by God.

That is, quite literally, the situation. The old-time, blue-blooded aristocracy of the city supports the " Watch and Ward Society "; several Lowells and Cabots contribute their money to keep my Socialist novel from reaching the common people of their city. And when I left Boston and returned to New York, the first sight I saw was a stack of my books, four feet high, in front of one of the news-stands in Grand Central station; I inquired of the clerk, and learned that this stack would last one day, and the cause of its rapid disappearance was people from Boston who took a copy home with them.

Besides the blue-bloods, who put up the money, there are two forces actively concerned, Catholic Mediævalism and Protestant Fundamentalism : the Knights of Columbus marching arm in arm with the Ku Klux Klan, and Cardinal O'Connell embracing Billy Sunday.   And do not fool yourself with the idea that there is anything peculiar to Boston in this combination of bigotries.   The same forces exist everywhere in America, and the Boston crowd are hell-bent to extend their methods to New York, so as to stop the flow of prohibited books.   If they can have their way, it means the end of modern literature in America; so it is worth while to understand the Boston law and the methods of enforcing it.

The secretary of the Watch and Ward Society was the Rev. J. Frank Chase, and so long as he lived, the suppression of books was done in silence.   Chase would tell the chairman of the booksellers' committee what books he objected to, and the booksellers would quietly take these books from their shelves.   The chairman of this committee, proprietor of the biggest bookstore in Boston, explained to me the Rev. Chase's moral standards.   Said Chase : " It's all right for the novelist to say that John went to bed with Mary, and Mary had a baby.   But the moment he shows John making any gesture towards Mary, tending to rouse her feelings, then the book is obscene, and I ban it."   Imagine, if you can, what would become of the courtship scenes of the world's literature, subjected to such a test !   Imagine what would happen, if such a censor were to stumble upon a copy of " Love's Pilgrimage "!

Rev. Chase died, and the police and the booksellers, lacking his divine guidance, got into a dispute, and that is how the present situation arose, with so much free advertising for " An American Tragedy " and " Elmer Gantry " and " Oil! "   But a truce has just been arranged, and the voice of God will again prevail

[171]

in Boston's book business.   The Watch and Ward Society
has got a new secretary, the Rev. Charles Bodwell, and
a reporter asked this gentleman what he thought of
Upton Sinclair's idea that the Bible and Shakespeare are
obscene under the Massachusetts law; he answered:
" Certain paragraphs in both books should be cut out
of editions that are open to the general public."

This Massachusetts law is built like a bear-trap.   It
specifies any book " containing "; so they can pick out
any passage they don't like, without considering the whole
book.   The judge who issued the warrant in the case of
" Oil! " admitted to me that he had read only the
passages complained of by the police; and a lawyer who
stood nearby and heard the conversation was very much
excited, and offered to testify to this outrageous state of
affairs.   I replied by advising the lawyer to look up his
Massachusetts law.   Under this law, the judge was under
no obligation to read the book.   The instructions given
to a jury, and upheld by the Supreme Court of Massachusetts were: " You are not trying any book except
this, and only such parts of this as the government
complains of."   And in order to make quite certain that
there could be no fairness in the trial, the learned judge
went on: " It makes no difference what the object in
writing this book was, or what its whole tone is."

Finally, the test of literature is its effect upon the
young.   " Manifestly tending to corrupt the morals of
youth," says the law.   Modern writers are confined to
the juvenile department; they are not permitted to discuss
the problems of adult life from an adult point of view.
Some youth is easily corrupted—when it has been brought
up under Catholic or Fundamentalist auspices, and kept
in ignorance of the elementary facts of life.

The superintendent of police in Boston is a large
Catholic gentleman by the name of Mike Crowley.   He
was much excited about my book, and told my lawyer
that it was " the worst of the lot," and that if I sold a
copy in Boston, he would personally appear to prosecute

me, and ask the judge to give me a year on Deer Island.
So I went to call on this official, and sold him a copy of
my book in his headquarters, and incidentally we had
a discussion, completely revealing as to the Catholic point
of view. I can't quote it all, because Mr. Crowley was
obscene in his description of obscenity. But he demanded
to know why we writers had suddenly taken to putting
such things into books. " It's only in the last few years
you've been doing it! "

" Surely, Mr. Crowley," I said, " you can't be very
familiar with standard literature. Shakespeare, for
example——"

" You don't find any of these bedroom scenes in
Shakespeare."

" Have you ever happened to read ' Cymbeline,' Mr.
Crowley? "

" Oh now, of course, you can put it over me in an
argument about books. But there's terrible things in that
book of yours, Mr. Sinclair."

" What, for example? "

" Isn't that the book in which the girl says that she
can have a lover, because her mother has one, and she
knows it? "

" Yes, that's in there."

" Well now, is that the kind of thing to be putting
into a book? "

" It happens to be a real case, Mr. Crowley. I knew
the people."

" Well, there might be such people, I don't deny, but
that's no reason for spreading the story. Such things
destroy the reverence that young girls ought to feel for
their mothers, and such things ought to be hushed up,
and not put into books for girls to read." And there,
of course, we had to part company, because I am in the
business of putting the facts about America into books.

The crucial fact about this censorship is that they
enforce their juvenile standards against modern writers,
and not against the classics. The police of Boston have

become very " cagy "; you cannot sell them " The
Scarlet Letter," nor any other old book they have been
warned about.   Seeking to bring out this point, I invited
them to a public meeting, and read them Act iii, Scene 2
of Hamlet, with its indubitably obscene language, and
invited them to buy the book; but they sat motionless.
I read them Genesis xix. 30-38, the quite horrible story
of Lot and his daughters.   Imagine, if you can, a modern
novel telling how two women get their father drunk
and then cohabit with him and bear him children!   I
offered this obscene book to the Boston police, but again
they would not enforce the law.   I sold it to a Boston
rationalist, who later applied for a warrant for my arrest
—and did not get it!

Then I held up a copy of " Oil! " before the police.
At least, it appeared to be " Oil! " and they bought it
promptly.   After they had notified me to appear in court
next morning, and had gone out, I called the attention
of the audience to the fact that I hadn't told the police
what the book was, and that what they had bought was
a copy of the Bible bound in the covers of " Oil! "   It
seemed to me that the way to meet this censorship was
with laughter, and the audience agreed with me—I have
never heard more hearty laughter from a crowd.   But
alas, the story had to reach the public through the " Brass
Check " press.   The three reporters who handled the
assignment were named Quinn, Shay, and Murphy; and
they held a conference—so I was told by one of the
newspaper photographers who attended.   Were they going
to let any smart-Aleck Socialist make a monkey out of
Mike Crowley?   They were not!   And they did not!

Next day I sold a real copy of " Oil! " to Mr. Crowley,
and again I was under temporary arrest.   But when I
appeared in court, I learned that the judge wouldn't have
me.   " We think, Mr. Sinclair, you've had your share
of book-advertising."   He was not on the bench when he
said this, so I could hit back.   " Look here, Judge Creed,
who started this advertising? You have advertised my book

as obscene, and certainly I'm going to advertise it as not
obscene! " But again I confronted the problem of the
" Brass Check " press. When I delayed to get arrested,
they called me a coward; and when I couldn't get arrested,
they said I had been foiled in my effort to be a martyr!

For sale in this pious city of Boston I prepared some
special copies of " Oil! " known as the " fig leaf edition."
The police object to pages 193-4-5-6, 203-4, 206, 328-9—a
total of nine pages out of 527. I had these pages blotted
out with a large black fig leaf, and I made sandwich
signs in the shape of a white fig leaf, labelled " Oil!
Fig Leaf Edition. Warranted 100% Pure under Boston
Law." I put on these signs, and sold the book all day
on the streets of Boston; if there was going to be any
more arresting, I wanted to be the prisoner. But there
was no arresting, and the " fig leaf edition " is now
being sold all over the country—since the bookstores
regard it as a " collector's item "!

The trial of the bookseller's clerk comes off in the fall,
and I expect to be there to defend him. Whether I will
be heard is uncertain, owing to the amiable provision of
the law, that " intent " does not matter. You may write
a novel about a sin, and portray your hero as spending
the rest of his life atoning for the sin, but that does not
help you; they pick out the sin, and condemn you on
that, and under the law neither judge nor jury knows
about the atonement. Theodore Dreiser's hero atones in
the electric chair, but even so, they have convicted a book-
clerk of the crime of selling " An American Tragedy."
And that is the law they want to impose upon the rest
of America!

I am finishing these proofs in September, and next
month there is to be a jury trial of the book-clerk who
sold " Oil! " I shall be there, to testify if I am allowed
to; and incidentally I expect to gather material for a new
novel, to be entitled " Boston," and to deal with the
Sacco-Vanzetti case. I suppose it is not against the law
to gather material about Boston in Boston. We shall see!

CHAPTER XXXVII

THE TENSION OF FRIENDSHIP

I COME now to a writer who has done me the great honour
to write my biography while I am alive. He has done
it with wisdom, insight, and superhuman sweetness of
temper, considering the many provocations I have given
him. Naturally, I am grateful, and disposed to repay
the debt: but this is not the place to do it. For purposes
of the present chapter, I shall pretend that Floyd Dell
is my worst enemy, and discuss his work as I should
do in that case: that is, by saying exactly what I think
about it, with no regard to personalities.

For fifteen years I have been saying that Floyd Dell
is the best critic of books in America. He has taste and
discrimination, wide reading, and skill in dissecting the
purpose of a writer. He knows two fields which are
closed to most men of letters—modern psychology and
revolutionary economics. Because of this, he can understand and judge where others merely fumble. Because
of it, I pay him the compliment of being willing to read
any book he praises.

That is enough for one man. But Floyd is also known
as a novelist, and earns his living that way. So long as
he is dealing with his own type of mind, the sensitive
artist bewildered by the world and having a hard time
getting adjusted to it, I follow him with the same interest
that I give to his personal talk. But when he goes out
from the play-world of adolescence to the real world of
grown men and women—up to date he has not gone
very far.

THE TENSION OF FRIENDSHIP

The main concern of adolescent artists is their sexual adjustments; and in Floyd's novels they have much adjusting to do, and take much time for it. We have had vehement arguments on this question—it seems rather comical, just now when I am being advertised by the Boston police as the chief of sinners in this respect, that I should for so long have been taking the view of the police against my best of friends! Yet so it was, a few years ago, in the case of " Janet March "; I contributed a review to the Hearst Sunday supplements, saying in substance that Janet was a young lady who did nothing for her keep, that her sex-code would expose her to venereal disease, and that her creator, in failing to mention such a possibility, was failing in his duty to youth. Soon after that the district attorney of New York got busy, and Janet was listed among those items for which the collectors pay ten or twenty dollars. Floyd's wife, my friend Marie Gage, was cross with me, as almost any human wife would be, and I was extremely uncomfortable, not having desired such an outcome. Later on, when I trusted Floyd as a biographer, Marie called me a bold man!

The question we debated on that occasion, and which we never shall settle, is this: to what extent does the reader gather that Janet March is admired by her creator, and presented as an ideal to be followed? Floyd denied that he intended such an impression; while I had got it, and so had others. I think the explanation lies in that quality which makes the excellence of Floyd as a critic; his impressionability, and willingness to give himself up to others. He gave himself up to Janet while he was writing her; and when I began to quarrel with her, he gave himself, just a little bit, to me.[1]

[1] Floyd Dell's comment on this:
Does this make any clearer my attitude towards Janet? I am fond of her, in my book, and in real life when I come across her; certainly I admire her courage and robustness; but for the neurotic twists which condemn her to so much pain and unhappiness I have pity and sympathy. The truth is that I feel about her love-affairs much as I felt about

Count Keyserling, the German philosopher, has written a book about marriage, setting forth that the aim of the institution is not happiness, but a tension. Perhaps the same idea applies to friendship; Floyd and I argue and fight, and each of us gets a new point of view. I received a letter from him, apropos of my chapter on James Branch Cabell in this volume, the sort of letter which a hundred years ago would have been preliminary to a duel; the substance of it was " It's a god-damned lie and a libel." So I changed the text a little, and put in a paragraph recording Floyd's opinion, and then we went to dinner, much pleasanter than a duel.

I have begged Floyd to deal with grown-up affairs—for example, those days when he sat in the prisoner's dock, facing a jury and a twenty-year jail sentence for opposition to the war. He made a try at it in " An Old Man's Folly," a story which entertained me in a peculiar way, since I appear as two characters in it! I can't get others to admire this novel as much as I do, so I am forced to

those of the hero of a recent work of mine entitled " Upton Sinclair " —and do you suppose I want people to do the absurd things *he* did? I do not hold people up to admiration—I haven't found any yet whom I could admire without any pity or any amusement. I tell their stories as truly as I can, believing in my didactic way that such stories are instructive to the young. I also believe the stories in the Old Testament to be instructive to the young and I have found nobody there to admire very much. In fact, I might confess that the Book of Judges is as much as anything else my literary model: and its final remark might be the motto of all my fiction:

" In those days there was no king in Israel: every man did that which was right in his own eyes." Or, as a modern translator puts it: " and everyone did exactly as he pleased."

Let me try again: If you know me, you know that I am a Utopian, and believe with all my heart in the possibility of human happiness: and when have I described a happy person? I know unhappiness so much better! When I find out how people should behave to be happy, then I will write a book and hold that conduct up to admiration and emulation. It will probably be a frightful bore—but I will do it. One word more: you do not state the age at which people become " grown-up," and cease to concern themselves with sexual adjustment. I think you really should tell me and your readers what that age is.

Yours maliciously,
FLOYD.

admit that perhaps, knowing the people in real life, I read too much between the lines.

Floyd Dell is young; the best of his life is before him, and great events are on the way, subjects for great fiction; perhaps he will deal with them. In any case, I value a keen and sensitive mind, swayed by all winds of thought, yet controlled by a rigid ideal of fair play and truth-telling.

CHAPTER XXXVIII

PAVEL JERDANOVITCH

THIS book is supposed to deal with writers only; but it so happens that I have been privileged for many years to know a great painter, one whose revolutionary impulse may remake American art, and it seems to me the reader will welcome a brief chapter about such a man.

Pavel Jerdanovitch is his name, and you will not need to ask the land of his nativity. He spent many years among the cannibals of the South Sea Islands, from which he derives his directness of approach to the goal of his desires. Now he lives in Hollywood, defending himself as best he can against the cannibals of commercialism. He began his painting only a few years ago, and I was present at the birth of his impulse, and saw his first masterpiece in becoming. Now his fame is international —his work has been exhibited in Chicago and New York, and has won the plaudits of eminent critics in Paris.

The most conspicuous aspect of this master's work is daring in the use of colour. It was John Ruskin who first taught me to enjoy colour in painting; I had been brought up on the pastel shades of the decadents, but Ruskin pointed out to me that strong and elemental souls love the brilliant primary colours, of which nature herself has been so lavish. The most famous of Pavel Jerdanovitch's pictures is called " Aspiration," and shows a woman of his cannibal tribes—the new and modernized cannibals who apparently have washtubs and wear cotton prints. The woman herself is stout, and coloured like chocolate caramels; she wears a red turban with large black spots, and a yellow dress with what appear to be blue snails on it. She has what is known in the technicalities of high art as " a Gaugin eye "; that is to say, a front face eye set in a profile, which is rather startling until you have accustomed yourself to the conventions of the new art. She has a blue tub full of white soap-suds, and all about her is vivid green grass, and mauve mountains crowned by a supernally blue sky. In front of the woman sits a large red bird, having green wings with white stripes and a yellow tail. From a clothes-line there wave two black socks, also a merry shirt, pink on one side and blue on the other—the kind they are making now for sale to the cannibal trade. Behind the washerwoman is her house, which is white, with a red chimney and a yellow roof, and alongside it stands a cosmos tree with great white leaves. Close behind the woman stands a cerise-coloured milking-stool, and on it rests her purse; a dark shadowy hand reaches out for it, but the woman does not notice, because her Gaugin eye is cast up to the bright-coloured bird in front of her.

That is why the picture is called " Aspiration," and you cannot really understand it unless you have been privileged, as I have been, to hear the master himself expound it. The bird is called the " cosmic rooster," and is a symbol of suppressed desires; it sits upon a cross, which is, of course, another symbol, and at the other end of the clothes-line is the cosmos flower with white leaves, signifying immortality. The entire painting affords a marvellous illustration of the law of dynamic symmetry; everything directs the eye of the beholder towards the central symbol, so that at first we are like the washerwoman, and fail to notice the hand of greed reaching for her purse. It is only after study and thought that we discover another stroke of genius : the only objects in the picture which cast a shadow are those which are intended to have mystical significance.

[181]

In short, this masterpiece of painting is a bit of hilarious absurdity, slapped on to canvas by my friend Paul Jordan Smith, who, besides being a novelist and scholar, is a satirist and wag. He sat himself down before an easel, without knowing any more about painting than I do, and proceeded to caricature the rubbish which for the past fifteen or twenty years has been palmed off on the public as " futurist " and " primitive " art. Having finished his labours, he hung the result on his study wall, and said nothing; and presently his friends began to stare and ask questions. Paul Jordan, in his spirit of waggery, began to take it seriously; he evolved his " spiel " about the " cosmic rooster " and the " law of dynamic symmetry," and he found that, in the parlance of the advertising experts, it " went over."

So then he decided to become an international figure, and invented the romantic " Pavel Jerdanovitch," with the Russian birth and the life among the cannibals. He had photographs of himself taken, dark and ferocious of aspect, and wild of eye. He painted three additional horrors—one called " Exaltation," portraying the ecstasies of a native damsel who summons up the courage to defy the tribal taboo and eat the sacred banana; another called " Adoration," portraying a savage worshipping a piebald boa-constrictor in Alaska, and a third called " Illumination," because it is made up almost entirely of eyes. " Exaltation " was crated and shipped to New York, where it was shown at the Independent Exhibit, in the Waldorf-Astoria Hotel, March, 1925, and solemnly discussed by the critics, and made the subject of an elaborate article in a Paris art journal, *Revue du Vrai et du Beau,* September 10, 1925, page 18. The picture of the washerwoman and the cosmic rooster was shown at the " No-Jury Exhibit," at Marshall Field's, in Chicago, January-February, 1926; and in the *Art World* of Tuesday, January 26, you will find a feature article, proclaiming this as the most brilliant exhibit of many moons. Out of the 480 pictures in the said brilliant exhibit, the great art journal selected for reproduction just one, and what do you think it was? " Aspiration," by Pavel Jerdanovitch! The cosmic rooster!

So once more the fame of the great cannibal painter reached Europe; he was appraised and celebrated in *Les Artistes D'Aujourd'hui*, and in *La Revue Moderne*, June 30, 1927, pages 18 and 19. This most exalted of art-magazines reproduces the cosmic rooster, and also the boa-constrictor in Alaska, and it says, among a lot of assorted praise: " Constructed on a large scale, in masses, with care to mark the contrasts rather than the exact perspective, the paintings of Jerdanovitch have a decorative character which is very interesting, and which approaches them sometimes to the paintings of Cezanne in the new manner. Moreover the post-impressionists are among the spiritual masters of our painter, notably Gaugin," etc.

Magazines pass, but books endure; and " our painter " has achieved immortality in a sumptuous volume—I lack words to tell how elegant it is, but many painters would sell one of their Gaugin eyes to be included in it. The title is: " L'Art Contemporain: Livre D'Or: Avec Une Preface de M. Gabriel Moussac; Paris." I open it, and behold, a full-page reproduction of the cosmic rooster, " Aspiration, par Pavel Jerdanovitch." And on the adjoining page a text, which I translate:

" A seeker and an unquiet spirit, he cannot content himself with the beaten paths. He has done some beautiful portraits, then some strange symbolical works, very beautiful: ' Exaltation,' ' Illumination,' ' Aspiration,' compositions very personal, where the art represents things in symbolizing the sentiments, from an angle which belongs to him, and which classes him altogether among the best artists of the advance-guard by a formula excluding all banality."

I don't see how anything could be funnier than this; and Paul Jordan thought the artists of America would appreciate a joke on their French confrères. Being invited to address the Art Association of Laguna Beach, where a company of our California artists gather to paint sky and clouds and sea, he told them about this hoax; and how did they take it? They were horrified at his act of blasphemy, and their leading critic published a review in the local newspaper, which for virulence outdoes anything I ever read, even about my blasphemous self. The critic even declared that Paul Jordan had got away with the proceeds of the lecture—the fact being that the association had charged fifty cents admission and paid the lecturer nothing!

The creator of " Pavel Jerdanovitch " is a novelist—so, in introducing him, I have not departed from the programme of my book. His first novel was called " Cables of Cobweb," and I suspect it is his own story, about a youth who grew up in Virginia, and escaped into the radical movement, but in the end went back to his ancestors. Paul Jordan has not gone back in person, but has gone a part of the way in spirit. Twenty years ago he was selling " The Jungle " from a soap-box in Chicago; but now he has lost his faith in the workers, and his hope for the salvation of his country, and devotes his time to reading James Joyce and James Branch Cabell, and writing expositions of their esoteric significance. And when I ridicule his idols, he is pained—exactly as the Laguna artists were pained by the blasphemous " Pavel Jerdanovitch "!

CHAPTER XXXIX

THE TRAMP POET

TWENTY-ONE years ago I came upon some verses by a young poet, then a student at the University of Kansas, to which he had come as a bare-footed tramp. In those verses I found what seemed to me the greatest promise for American poetry in my time. I wrote to this youth, and he became my friend; I have a volume of his letters, strange, wild outpourings from a poet drunken without wine, a true child of the muses, who needed only nature and his own soul for company. Harry Kemp lived as his forbears of the great tradition lived, upon bread and cheese, sleeping in a garret, with a horse-blanket for a cover. He read these great forbears, and roamed the fields, and sang with ecstasy, and came home and wrote until dawn; his letters would break into verse, pouring itself out for pages, really good poetry, spontaneous and unrevised. Among his class-mates at the university he was a strange freak of nature; every few months he would fall madly in love with some college damsel, and write me a heartbroken farewell, and detail his plans for suicide.

Something happened to this young poet. It is not for me to discuss the matter : suffice it to say that what had been the pure ecstasy of art became all at once the poisoned brew of sensuality. In his first book, " The Cry of Youth," the poems are all jumbled together, but it is easy to sort them out. Wherever the poet is writing of the stars and the winds, the mighty works of men and the march of science, you know it belongs to his first period; when he is writing about ladies who bite blood from the lips of their lovers, it belongs to his second.

The facts preach their own lesson and I am not the one to elaborate it. The great promises which Harry Kemp made to American literature were not kept. No longer does he prophesy the glories that are to be; he is content to echo the cynicisms of the cafés. To be sure, he has written an entertaining autobiography; but I say that it is one thing to write poetry, and another to write about writing it.

This poet confesses his sins with uncustomary frankness, and for a while that disarms us; until we come to understand that he means to go on with these sins, in order to have material for more confessions. Reflecting upon this view of life, I recall something from the volume of Mormon propaganda, which I am carrying back to California in my suit-case. It will amuse Harry to hear what the Angel Moroni thinks of him; so here is the second of the " Leaves from the Tree of Life " by Charles W. Penrose, member of the First Presidency of the Church of Jesus Christ of Latter Day Saints:

" Repentance . . . includes sorrow for the past and determination for the future. The first of these without the second is not genuine repentance. It is barren and fruitless, and is therefore unacceptable to God. Resolutions of future rectitude are naturally accompanied by grief for past wrong-doing, but regret may exist without reform, and such is not saving repentance, the virtue of which is in turning from evil and cleaving to good. Tears, self-reproaches, lamentations, self-abasement in language or in gesture do not constitute repentance, no matter how loudly they may be indulged in or how conspicuous they may appear, but it is evidenced by forsaking things one knows to be wrong and practising that which one is satisfied is right. Humility is one of its chief characteristics and this prompts obedience."

This is funny; but it does not dispose of Harry Kemp, nor of my grief for the promises he made and broke. I prefer to think of him as the tramp poet of those happier days, living over a stable in Lawrence, Kansas, and singing of

GOD, THE ARCHITECT

Who thou art I know not,
  But this much I know:
Thou hast set the Pleiades
  In a silver row;

Thou has sent the trackless winds
  Loose upon their way;
Thou hast reared a coloured wall
  'Twixt the night and day;

Thou hast made the flowers to blow
  And the stars to shine,
Hid rare gems and richest ore
  In the tunnelled mine—

But, chief of all thy wondrous works,
  Supreme of all thy plan,
Thou hast put an upward reach
  In the heart of Man!

CHAPTER XL

THE DAYS DEPARTED

THERE was another tramp poet in that happy age. He wandered over the country with a bundle of " Rhymes to be Traded for Bread," and he made strange ecstatic drawings of his native town, which was going to become better than it was. Being hungry for a better America, and for young poets to make it so, I became a friend to Vachel Lindsay, and cheered him up and up—like a sky-rocket. We met in New York, and it was a queer session; sitting at lunch, he eyed me anxiously for a while, and suddenly broke out, " You're disappointed, I don't look the way you thought I would! " It was true in a way, for Vachel doesn't appear the poet, except that he has a wild eye; the rest of him might be any well-ordered young business man.

I am disappointed nowadays, and have told him so, because I can see little purpose or meaning in the things he contributes to our highbrow magazines. Long ago I suggested to him a theme for one of his chants—the Soap-box. He promised to do it, and years later I reminded him of his promise and he told me that he had written the poem; I had read it, and hadn't known what it was about! Among my requirements for poetry are that it shall lie within the limits of my understanding; if it does not, I leave it for more subtle critics.

But I say of Vachel what I said of Harry Kemp; what he writes now does not alter what he wrote years ago, and will not count against him in the final reckoning. He has given us one of our great radical poems, the tribute

to Governor Altgeld, " Sleep softly . . . eagle forgotten
. . . under the stone." And " The Congo " is a thing
of glory, which needs nothing else to support it. Very
probably, as Floyd Dell has pointed out, its rhythm and
spirit were derived from Chesterton's " Lepanto "; but
that need not trouble us—all poets have to learn their
tricks, and if there were no origins and influences, there
would be nothing for the compilers of doctoral theses to
be learned about.

Vachel Lindsay as a man is worthy of honour. He has
lived for his high calling, and not soiled his name with
wantonness. He has earned a simple living by lecturing
and reading his poetry to audiences. I write of him here
as a comrade, and say only what I have said to him
personally when we meet. I plead with poets, as with
all other writers, to make use of the gigantic themes of
our time, the social struggles, and gropings of the masses
towards freedom. Also, I plead with them to write
simply, as the great writers have nearly always been
willing to do.

And much the same I have to report concerning
another Socialist poet, Carl Sandburg. I got a thrill out
of his early Chicago stuff, which I have failed to get from
his later writings. He is earning his living by contributing to the *Chicago Daily News*, and I understand
our newspapers too well to expect him to say much of
importance there. Just now, as I revise these proofs,
one of the most popular of American journalists, Hey-
wood Broun, is separated from the *New York World*,
for the offence of speaking the truth about the Sacco-
Vanzetti case.

American journalism has devoured one poet after
another whom I could name. I open a Sunday paper
and find James Oppenheim writing about psycho-analysis.
I have no quarrel with this subject, but I prefer Oppenheim
as the author of " Bread and Roses."

If we have a single poet in America who is able to
live by his poetry alone, I don't know who it can be,

except possibly Edgar Guest. Poets have to recite, and give lectures—the wandering minstrel, as of yore. It is an improvement that the minstrel is not drenched and storm-beaten, but arrives in a taxi-cab, and had his berth in the sleeping-car paid for by his lecture bureau. But the fact remains that a poet who has to travel with the bourgeoisie, and be displayed before them, comes automatically and unconsciously under the spell of our system of mass production, which operates upon men's minds as well as their bodies, and ordains that every man shall look like a tailor's advertisement, and shall think like the writer of the advertisement.

CHAPTER XLI

THE SOAP-BOX

Who are the American poets who write consciously and deliberately in the cause of labour? First among them I name Edwin Markham, who began when I was a youth, and has been at it ever since. His " Man with the Hoe " is old stuff, in the sense that we all know it, but it is none the less powerful for that. Markham has written a great deal, and we judge him by his average work; but in the end a poet's rank is always decided by his best work.

And then Arturo Giovannitti, whom once American capitalism attempted to " frame " and execute for murder, as penalty for leading a great strike. From that experience came a poem, " The Walker," which will not soon be forgotten. Since then Giovannitti has suffered from tuberculosis, which excuses him from further authorship. But as I revise these proofs, he is arrested with the little band of heroes who are picketing the State House in Boston, in futile protest against the murder of Sacco and Vanzetti. All honour to poets who are also heroes! And to those who, like Dorothy Parker and Edna Millay, are heroines! The latter of these women has shown us that it is possible to combine the ecstasy of pure poetry with social conscience and intelligence.

And then John G. Neihardt, who has become famous as a poet of the Indian wars, a school-book classic and poet-laureate of Nebraska—but without giving up his rebel soul. The Indians call him " Little Bull Buffalo," which is how he looks. Just recently he has had his

[191]

collected works published—and without omitting the
radical stuff.

And Ralph Chaplin, who went to jail for his I.W.W.
faith, and has not recanted.   When the great anthology
of American poetry is made up, you will find something
out of " Bars and Shadows " in it.   Also there will be
something from Margaret Widdemer and from Sarah N.
Cleghorn; and from James Larkin Pearson—do you know
that we have a sort of American Burns, living in a North
Carolina village and publishing his humble verses, set up
by his own fingers?   He isn't so free a man as Burns
—he still believes the wretched old Bible stuff, and has
joined the peculiar sect known as " Russellites."   But
then, he keeps sober and works hard; whereas Burns, the
complete rebel, got drunk and went to the devil.   The
dilemma we faced with the Mormons, you recall!   Make
note of Pearson's address, a town with the weird name
of Boomer; I will give you one of his poems, in the hope
that you may be moved to send two dollars for the book,
and help feed the poet.   He writes me that, at the moment
of writing, he owns three dollars and twenty cents.   Yet
he writes like this :

HOMER IN A GARDEN

A sheltered garden in a sheltered land,
   A pleasant seat upon the mossy ground;
A book of Homer open in my hand,
   And languorous sweet odours all around.

Then suddenly the ages fell away;
   My sheltered garden floated off in space;
And on some lost millennium's bloody day
   I stood with storied Ilium face to face.

The honeysuckle smells that would not fade
   Hung like a ghost above the field of red,
And every dreaming pansy-face was made
   The likeness of the faces of the dead.

Such wonders were abroad in all the land—
   Such magic did the mighty gods employ—
That every lily was a Helen's hand,
   And every rose a burning tower of Troy.

Also my friend Sam DeWitt. For ten years or more Sam has been contributing poems to the Socialist press of New York, and when a few days ago I mentioned his name to a literary comrade, I noted a patronizing smile. Sam went to the College of the City of New York, like me, and was tennis champion of the city a few times, and got kicked out of the state legislature for being a Socialist, and now is keeping the *New Leader* out of debt—and what has all that to do with poetry? Can any good thing come out of Nazareth?

I have his three little volumes in my suit-case, carrying them back to California in triumph, having won them in a tennis duel. I run through them, and notice at the outset, they contain one quality which constitutes an insurmountable barrier to poetic fame in our time—it is always possible to know exactly what they mean. You can see this fatal fault in the very opening lines of the volume called " Riding the Storm ":

> I chant such songs as never bring
>   A smile from fortune's face;
> And yet I am content to sing
>   And hold my lowly place.
>
> I have no praise or honeyed phrase
>   For glories that are gone;
> I only fill these darkened days
>   With sonnets to the dawn.

And then turn over a few pages, and you will observe that Sam is a preacher like me, abhorring waste, and trying to reform even the elements!

> If I were the March wind,
>   If I had his passion;
> I would not waste it
>   In his wanton fashion.
>
> I would not spend it
>   In idle emotions;
> Uprooting woodlands—
>   Lashing the oceans. . . .
>
> If I were the March wind,
>   If I held his passion:
> I would find use for it
>   In a grim fashion.

Also I will tell you about one Socialist poet whom you can't read, because I own the only copy of his work in the world.   Gerald Lively is his name, and he sent me his manuscript, and then, because America was starving him and his wife and babies, he went away to the Argentine, and may be dead for all I know.   " Songs of a Soil Slave " is the un-American and unpatriotic title which Gerald selected for his verses, and I wrote an article about them for *Pearson's Magazine,* and a rich young man of my acquaintance agreed to finance their publication, but failed to do so.   Now the Vanguard Press offers to bring them out if I can raise five hundred dollars; so I give a couple of samples, to see if there is anyone who cares that much for a new voice of the workers.   And maybe Gerald will hear about it and write and tell me where he is.

Here is the soil slave's vision of his children :

> Sad and weary little figures,
>   Drenched and sodden in the rain,
> Driving cows in from the pasture,
>   Herding cattle from the grain.
>
> They're not playing in the hayfields,
>   Weary, trailing little feet;
> Where's the game for little children,
>   Pulling mustard in the wheat?

And again, here is a soil slave's religion; it was in 1915, and he had read how the people of Europe were turning to faith again, and it moved him to reflection, as follows :

> Thou, whose red hand hath blazed a path
>   The crimson ages down—
> Thou comest to thine own again
>   With blood upon thy crown.
>
> The war-worn peoples in despair
>   Turn backward to the slime,
> And cast before thy feet of clay
>   The wasted work of Time.
>
> The wider creeds that we believed
>   Fall to the tribal law;
> The gentler gods we could have loved
>   Are 'neath thy fang and claw.
>
> The darkness to the darkness calls,
>   A monotone of pain;
> But thou, the God of Sabaoth,
>   Reignest on earth again

CHAPTER XLII

HOMO UNIUS LIBRI

THE pathway of my life is strewn with the wrecks of literary hopes: young writers who promised great novels, and then failed to keep the promise. I have named a few of them—Herbert Quick, who wrote " The Broken Lance," and George Cram Cook, who wrote " The Chasm," and Ernest Poole, who wrote " The Harbour," and Arthur Bullard, who wrote two vivid stories, " A Man's World " and " Comrade Yetta." For many years I used to wonder why a man should hide such a talent under a pen name. Now I wonder whether it was that he possessed clairvoyant gifts, and was able to foresee that he was going to turn his back upon the working-class movement, and give his aid to the interventionists who were seeking to destroy the Russian revolution.

And what has become of I. K. Friedman, who wrote a stirring novel of the steel industry, " By Bread Alone "? And of " Jimmie " Hopper, who wrote " Goosie," that charming tale, in the early Wells manner, about a young poet who began to grow wings, and the terrible embarrassment it was to his family, and how his wife insisted on trimming his feathers. A cry of anguish was in that little story, echoing out of the wilderness of American respectability.

I remember also an early novel called " Quicksand," by Hervey White. This, too, was the tale of a young writer's futile effort to save his soul. Charlotte Perkins Gilman used to rave over that book, and for a while I kept in touch with the author, who was teaching country school for a living, and turning into an eccentric—one of the tragic fates which befall talent that is lonely and without group support. He sent me the manuscript of another novel, written in a prose style quite maddening to read, with whole paragraphs which scanned as blank verse.

There is a certain type of mind which can produce one worthwhile novel, the story of the writer's own life. The things he has actually seen and felt, he can make us see and feel; but when he tries to create new characters, they do not come to life. Such a writer was my friend Dell Munger; you will hunt a long time for a more vivid story of the life of a farm-woman on the prairies than " The Wind Before the Dawn." And Hjalmar Rutzebeck's extraordinary adventures in the far North, " Alaska Man's Luck "; and Ed Morrell's dreadful experience, " The Twenty-fifth Man," and Jack Black's story of the underworld, " You Can't Win." Here is the raw stuff of American life, from which students of the future will learn what our society was really like.

There are persons who are doing work which they consider of more importance than novel-writing. Abraham Cahan is editing the " Forwards," and educating all the Jews of New York. So " The Rise of David Levinsky " remains his one masterpiece—a picture of Jewish success in America, dead sea fruit which turns to ashes on the lips. It is curious to note, this Russian-Hebrew editor of the New York slums gives exactly the same report as a native-born writer on the other side of the continent, Charles G. Norris, who tells us in " Pig Iron " about a native youth who makes all the kinds of success there are in America, and at the end is wandering around in a palace, discontented because he cannot get some fool station on the radio.

And Mr. and Mrs. Haldeman-Julius, also too busy to write novels, having a weekly and a monthly and a quarterly to edit, and millions of little blue books to get out every year. To break down the bigotry of American Fundamentalism is a worthy work, so all I can say is that if they ever write another novel like " Dust," I will read it. Here in the centre of the continent, exactly half-way between Cahan and Norris, success turns out to be the same empty and unsatisfying thing!

[196]

CHAPTER XLIII

A FRIEND IN NEED

THERE are other novelists who are sticking to their jobs, and upon whom my hopes are centred. I begin with one whom I know well, and to whom I cannot pay enough tribute. Twenty-two years ago she came to be my secretary on a farm near Princeton—a quiet, unpretentious little woman, red-haired and bespectacled, and glad of a refuge from the maulings of fate. She had been a wage-slave of the Standard dictionary, and her eye-sight was ruined, and her life a torment as a result. When you got to know her you discovered that she could observe, and understand what she saw, and her sly sense of humour could become a weapon of defence in case of need. But no one knew she was a genius—I doubt if she knew it herself.

We took her to Helicon Hall, and there she met Allan Updegraff, a young poet, whom later she married. " Up " was there as Sinclair Lewis's chum, and those three had a little table in our dining-hall, and doubtless did no end of laughing at the queer assortment of humans about them. It was a laboratory for writers—I count ten who were then known or have since become so. Edith and " Up " parted, and she married a working-man and went to live with him in the tobacco country of Kentucky. So we have one of the classics of American fiction, " Weeds," by Edith Summers Kelley.

I do not know of any quality which a novel of working-class life could have which this novel lacks. It has grace of style, dignity of manner, intensity of feeling, exactness of observation, and depth of insight. It has beauty, tenderness, wisdom; yet it is nothing but the story of a young country couple, tenant farmers, who struggle and suffer and fail, as a million of the soil-slaves of America failed last year. It is certainly an enduring book, but I am not content to have it recognized by the next generation. I want it to be recognized now, so that its author can write other books. Edith's husband is a wage-earner, and she has two children to protect from capitalist America; also, she is half blind. " Me," she writes, in a letter not meant for the public—" me, I am as discouraged as a wet caterpillar. For nearly a year I have been taking an eye-cure, and although I have made a great deal of progress, I am still a long way from being able to read with any sort of ease. Just think, for nearly a year I have read absolutely nothing. My daughter, who is now fifteen, occasionally reads aloud a little of an evening and that is all. I am getting so dead for lack of mental stimulation that I sometimes wonder if I can ever come to life again."

Having been myself at various times both poor and ill, I am aware that fine words butter no literary parsnips. I write this in the hope that someone will not merely get " Weeds " and recognize a proletarian masterpiece, but will take steps to see that Mrs. Kelley gets the help she needs. She has another book under way; and all my life I have been willing to do unconventional things to save a worthwhile book, my own or another's. Great books are the seeds of the future, and the most important things we have in our world.

CHAPTER XLIV

THE REBEL BAND

ANOTHER young writer once lived in my home; he gave me
help in compiling " The Cry for Justice "—raising the devil
because of my bad taste in admiring Edward Carpenter,
and making me acquainted with the three coming poets of
America, " Jimmie Opp," " Louie Unt," and himself.
Inasmuch as he had just composed a sonnet which I have
declared as good as Milton's best, he did not seem presumptuous to me. You can find the sonnet in " Mammonart," also in " The Cry for Justice "; it was addressed to
young Mr. Rockefeller, at the time of the Ludlow massacre,
and you may be sure the " rich young ruler " regrets
having earned immortality in that fashion.

One other great ambition haunted Clement Wood in
those far-off ante-bellum days; he wanted to beat me at
tennis, and the ambition kept him busy a whole summer.
In his spare hours he wandered over the hills of Croton,
bellowing the chants of Vachel Lindsay in tones which
shook the leaves off the chestnut trees. Since then he has
written several novels: one of them, " Mountain," a vivid
picture of the class struggle in the new industrial South,
from which the author comes, and where he was a justice
of the peace before he was of age. You can always get a
" rise " out of him by hailing him as " Judge," in
Southern style.

Clement is jolly, and such good company that it is hard
for me to remember my promise, to put my friends on
equal terms with my worst enemies in this book. Why is it

that Clement's work has not achieved the greatness of his early promise? I think the answer is that his make-up contains a greater share of ambition than of sincerity. When it has come to the show-down he has been unwilling to pay the penalties which great art exacts. Just before he wrote his sonnet, " To a Rich Young Ruler," he withdrew from our Broadway demonstration, telling us that he had a job he was unwilling to jeopardize. During the war, he became a Quaker—and only during the war. Since then, to earn a living, he has written " little blue books " on such subjects as " How to Kiss "—and his kisses were of a kind which the muse of Milton would have spurned. So I have to remind my friend of Goethe's stern admonition, that the heavenly powers are revealed only to those who have eaten their bread with tears.

Next I mention John Dos Passos, genial and restless wanderer. He did not like the army, and gave us " Three Soldiers," which is a classic of the anti-militarist movement, the hope of civilization. Recently he published a *magnum opus*, " Manhattan Transfer," and three days ago he stood on a street corner and listened with great patience while I compared it to a kaleidoscope. He tried to give us, in a series of swift pictures, a sense of the confusion and rush of New York; and for me he gave it too well. There are a dozen characters in " Manhattan Transfer " whose stories I wanted to follow, but I got transferred from one to another so many times that I lost track of them all. My plea to Dos Passos, standing on the street corner of his bewildering Manhattan, was to write a plain, straightaway novel with the same emotional power and radical insight, and thus join our best-sellers.

Also W. E. Woodward, a person with a charming satiric touch. Mr. Woodward took the precaution to make a success in the business world before he broke loose, and so did his wife, and from these two no innermost sacred shrine of the great temple of Bunk remains veiled. Just a little more story interest he will have to put into his fiction, if the great reading public is to discover him.

Meantime he remains what Ambrose Bierce was in the last generation, a pass-word to the elect.

And William C. Bullitt, who ten years ago was on everyone's tongue, because President Wilson sent him to Russia to make a report, and he and Lincoln Steffens broke the world's diplomatic record by telling the truth. Bullitt comes of one of the old families of Philadelphia, and might be one of Colonel Lorimer's darlings, but for the hard luck that he was born with a conscience. He is married to John Reed's widow, Louise Bryant, so he has a foot in both worlds, the respectable and the revolutionary; a fine strategic position for a writer.

He has given us a vital first novel, " It's Not Done." I know the highbrow critics call it melodrama, but that is merely their ignorance. The plain truth is that you cannot be melodramatic in writing about big business and smart society. The reality so far exceeds imagination that if you were Conan Doyle and Eugene Sue and Ouida and Alexandre Dumas all rolled into one, you could not keep up with the daily papers.

Also I owe mention to Charles Rumford Walker, whose novel, " Bread and Fire," appears while I am writing. Mr. Walker gently " kids " the ladies and gentlemen who are playing at being radicals; and that is all right, they can stand it. But also, Mr. Walker took the trouble to go and get a man-sized job in a copper-mill and see how it felt; so he has a real story to tell, and a true report of the class struggle. It happens that he can write, and he is a novelist to watch.

I don't know whether T. S. Stribling cares to travel in such company as this. He has written a novel, " Teeftallow," the story of a labourer among the hill people of Tennessee. It is simple, straightforward, affecting. Does Mr. Stribling merely report in cold blood what he sees? Or will he follow these humble wage-slaves when they waken to protest? I shall await developments, and not repeat the funny blunder I made in my youth, when I read " Esther Waters," and wrote a letter of burning enthusiasm, and received, to my bewilderment, a reply to the effect that English was dead as a language to write books in, and that Mr. George Moore was planning to use ancient Erse! It took years of study before I could comprehend the type of sensualist-æsthete, who would portray the sufferings of an English serving-maid as an exercise in technique, while spurning any practical step to help her out of degradation.

And Louis Bromfield, who has established himself as one of our younger novelists who can create character, and is striving to envisage the whole American scene. At first I thought he was too ardent an admirer of the charming and lovely rich; but his last novel, " A Good Woman," is as full of social protest as if I had written it myself. Slowly the soul of America is changing, and each day it becomes a little more difficult for a man of brains and conscience to remain indifferent to the knaveries and brutalities of what we call our civilization.

CHAPTER XLV

THE NEW PLAYWRIGHTS

ALSO there are young dramatists, holding up the banner of revolt. Five of them have organized as the " New Playwrights' Theatre," and got some backing, and as this book appears, they will be offering " Singing Jailbirds " in New York. It is the kind of thing these young radicals like to do, with a labour strike, and mob scenes, and plenty of music and expressionist effects. California will be agreeable to the production, on the well-established principle that every knock is a boost.

One of these New Playwrights is John Dos Passos. Another is Francis Faragoh, author of " Pinwheel." It is good social criticism, but rather a story in pictures than a drama; we miss the element of struggle, which makes a play. There is Em Jo Basshe, author of " Earth "; and John Howard Lawson, author of " Processional," a riot of American jazz and hilarity. Finally, Mike Gold, my favourite young genius for some years; he has an autobiographical novel about an East Side slum boy, which I find interesting, but which I can't persuade him to publish. Now he has a Mexican play, " Fiesta," which the New Playwrights are to produce; also he writes propaganda for the *New Masses*, and writes me letters, quarrelling with my messianic delusions—it is another of those tensions of friendship. I have to reply that I wouldn't in the least object to being a Messiah, if I could; I am sure the world needs one badly.

I have renewed my acquaintance with the New York drama, and observe that the Theatre Guild continues its custom of keeping us acquainted with the aristocratic depravities of Europe. Vienna knows how to be charming in its vileness, and this is what the high-powered rich of New York aspire to. I note that my friend Sidney Howard, who knows the labour movement, is compelled on the stage to resolve the domestic problems of the prosperous. Not long ago he presented us with a stage " wobbly " from California, who begot a child by another man's wife; they knew what they wanted, and their creator knew what the public must have. Broadway theatrical success continues to depend upon the enhancement of sexuality and the suppression of dangerous ideas. I suppose I ought to feel flattered by a remark made to me by my good friend Fulton Oursler, as he took me to see his mystery-play, " The Spider " : " My social conscience doesn't seem to be active except when I am reading one of your books ! "

Eugene O'Neill had the amusing idea of taking Sinclair Lewis's Babbitt and dressing him in mediæval costume, and sending him to China to talk like an American travelling salesman to the Grand Khan and his granddaughter. This version of Marco Polo will take five hours, and make trouble for the schedules of the suburban railroads.

Also, there was a play called " Spread Eagle "—extry! extry! all about our next war with Mexico! I missed it, but it ran for quite a while, and showed exactly how big business arranges its wars; at the end, when the actors waved the star-spangled banner, everybody felt exactly as patriotic as they will feel when it happens. Will Hays, czar of movies, has banned this play from the screen; also " An American Tragedy "—after the would-be producers had paid ninety thousand dollars for the rights! This little Presbyterian puppet of Wall Street is the undisputed master of our most important means of popular education, and the people are perfectly satisfied with what he is doing —or would be, if they knew anything about it!

CHAPTER XLVI

THE DOUBLE STANDARD

" Upton Sinclair's idea of literature is Socialist propaganda. If a book contains that, it's good, and if it doesn't, it's no good." Thus a young critic, reading these chapters in serial form.

Let me tell you a story. Four years ago the city of Los Angeles threw a thousand working-men into jail for the crime of being on strike; and I with a group of friends considered it a matter of duty to go and make a speech in defiance of the police edict. The story of this arrest was telegraphed to the East, and a certain writer, one of the most famous and prosperous of our humorists—I will call him Mr. X—referred to the matter in his weekly contribution to the Sunday newspapers; causing one of his humorous characters to remark to the other humorous character that I had taken this step as a means of obtaining publicity. It is a stock remark, which I have heard a thousand times in my life, and I paid no especial attention to it, understanding that a man who has to write two funny columns every seven days must occasionally be hard up for material.

But it happened that a month or so later this Mr. X came to California to spend the winter, and was a dinner-guest of the Pasadena Press Club, and I was invited to meet him. I went; and presently Mr. X was introduced by the chairman, and rose to make what everyone expected would be the conventional after-dinner speech, with plenty of comic stories. Instead of that he proceeded in a very grave tone to inform the assembled press men of the city that they had among them a first-class hero and major prophet, whom it was Mr. X's intention to honour that evening. This hero did not cringe like the rest of us before arrogant power, but took seriously his duties as a citizen of a free commonwealth; he had been willing to suffer arrest and imprisonment in order to defend the constitutional rights of humble working-men; and so on. In short, Mr. X was making a speech about myself, and the blood began to climb up the back of my collar and take lodgment in my ears, and I found myself with an intense desire to slide under the table and hide. But there stood Mr. X, speaking with such sincerity and intense feeling that presently he had all the diners applauding, and I had to get up and stammer a few words of thanks.

It was only after I got home and had time to think it over that I realized the extraordinary significance of this episode. You see, Mr. X has a double standard of judgment : one when he is among his friends and colleagues, and can say what he really thinks; and the other when he is earning his living, and saying what his paymasters require him to say. These two sets of judgments are contradictory and incompatible; and yet Mr. X can voice either one with impartial effectiveness.

Let me tell you another story. There is in Chicago a daily newspaper which for many years has made a pretence of liberalism—to the extent of saying that it is liberal. It publishes a book review section, and sends that page gratis to many publishers and authors, as a means of obtaining advertisements; so it happens that for ten years or so I have followed the literary life of Chicago. The editor of this page was a young critic, trying to build up a tradition and give himself a thrill by having a coffee-house and a coterie in the Addison-Steele-Old-English fashion. I had read about the group of young wits who assembled at this Chicago coffee-house, and it sounded romantic; so, happening to be in Chicago for an afternoon, I dropped in on this editor, and was taken to meet the gang. We sat around a table, and I ordered a glass of cider, and got a glass of warm vinegar, and we gossiped about books and writers, and presently the young editor warmed up to me. " Oh, yes, Sinclair, I read your books, you may be sure, even though I don't review them. ' The Goose-step ' "—and for a few minutes he sang the praises of " The Goose-step," at that time my latest book. " It made a great stir at the university, and I'd have liked to give it a good splurge, but you know how it is, I'd have got into trouble here on the paper, and what is the use? "

So here again the double standard of literary morals. This able young man understands the world he lives in— understands it so well that soon afterwards he was called to become literary editor of a leading newspaper of New York. I suppose he figured that he was doing no harm except to me—and I was used to it. What he failed to realize was that he was giving to the mass of his readers a false picture of current literature and life, and preventing American writers from performing their most important function. The result of this system of double standard in literary morals is that we have a nation sharply divided into a few thousand sophisticated and cynical intellectuals, and a hundred million pitiful ignoramuses, ready to swallow any fairy-tale that is told to them, and to run after any wretched fraud their masters choose to set up.

So you see, what the critics refer to as " Socialist propaganda " turns out upon investigation to be common honesty and intellectual freedom: the right of thinking men to voice their thoughts, without having a bludgeon held over their heads by some greedy commerical pirate who happens to have possessed himself of a chain of newspapers or magazines.

CHAPTER XLVII

THE ART OF BROTHERHOOD

I will go farther and say, it is not merely a question of common honesty, and freedom for the writer; it is a question of the fundamental nature of art. The purpose of art is to communicate the artist's emotions and view of life to others; and the impulse from which the act of creation proceeds is one of sympathy, of faith in the others, their ability to share these towering emotions, and their desire to do so. Otherwise, why undertake the labour, why endure the pangs of art creation? No, if you do not love your fellow-men, and desire the unfoldment of their beings, go into the business of speculating in real estate, and leave art alone. " Seid umschlungen, millionen! " exclaims Schiller, in his " Hymn to Joy "; " be ye embraced, O millions," and he didn't mean dollars, as we should mean in America.

Of course the great artist may know that the thing he is writing is beyond the immediate comprehension of the masses; he may be addressing an audience of his peers. But he must have the conviction that ultimately his message will reach the masses and affect their lives. All great artists have had this aim; Homer, Sophocles, Euripedes, Virgil, Dante, Cervantes, Shakespeare, Milton, Goethe, Byron, Hugo—such writers, despite the aristocratic elements in their make-up—wrote for mankind. Even one like Molière, who was tied by economic bonds to a court, wrote in such a way that his works became a scandal, and filtered down to strata of the population who were not supposed to know about the theatre. Even those who, like Aristophanes or Walter Scott, defend the aristocratic tradition, write for the purpose of holding the masses in line for that tradition; such is the basis of their appeal. Those writers who put the aristocratic tradition into actual effect, who really despise the masses, and decline to " cater to them "—such writers cherish in themselves the seeds of corruption, and are at once the symptom and cause of the breakdown of their society. For the brotherhood of man is a reality, and must be put into practice in a civilization, if that civilization is not to be wrecked by class conflicts.

Every civilization that has so far existed in the world has been aristocratic or plutocratic; it has repudiated brotherhood, and established slavery and exploitation, with the twin consequences of luxury at the top and misery at the bottom; and so it comes about that the great unsolved riddle of history is how to build a civilization that will endure. I find myself living in a country which is going ahead repeating the old blunders and crimes. I look at America—with my own eyes, not the coloured spectacles of the capitalist press—and I see in all essentials the same plutocracy I would have seen had I lived in ancient Rome.

I write this final chapter on a momentous day in the history of my country. Two big-muscled bruisers, elaborately trained for the purpose, are pounding each other into insensibility for a prize of a million dollars; and all the costly agencies of publicity in America are turned to giving the people a blow-by-blow account of this pounding, within a few seconds of its happening. Some hundreds of telegraph wires have been run to the spot, and reporters and messengers and telegraphers, working in relays, convey the news to printing presses in a thousand newspaper offices; likewise the radio systems of the country, with a few churchly exceptions, are hitched up together, and in ten thousand assembly halls and on street corners the vacant-minded mobs stand gaping, while a raucous voice shouts swiftly, " Sharkey jabs Dempsey a nasty upper-cut to the jaw—Dempsey lands a fierce wallop to the stomach "—and so on for an hour or so.

Understand, it is forbidden to use the radio to proclaim peace on earth and goodwill to men; again and again it has happened that a speaker, venturing to say a few words in opposition to the wholesale slaughter of human beings, has been cut off from his audience and left orating to the void. Systematically and continuously it happens all over America that the men and women who advocate justice and brotherhood are excluded from the air—the present writer, for example, has yet to enjoy the privilege, though large groups of persons have sought to hear him. But for the reporting of nasty upper-cuts to the jaw and of fierce wallops to the stomach the entire radio system of America is hooked up; and can anyone ask further proof of my thesis, that the masters of this country are drunk with greed, and willing to subject their wage-slaves to any degradation whatever, as a means of perpetuating the masters' power?

They may succeed; but only at the cost of destroying society. For capitalism carries within itself the seeds of its own death; it can produce wealth, but cannot distribute it, and the future of our world is like its past, a series of crises, with glutted markets and unemployment. For the moment we are on the crest of a wave of prosperity, and we think that all is well. But this prosperity is based upon the shipping of our surplus products abroad, and taking in return unlimited paper promises which can never be redeemed. When the time comes that men realize the worthlessness of these debts, our system of credit falls like a house of cards, and our people are out of work again. The remedy is another war to take away the markets from some rival nation. Thus the destiny of the workers under capitalism is to breed new generations, to fight new wars, to win new opportunities of profit for their masters. With the improvement of the technique of slaughter, each war becomes more horrible to contemplate, and worse yet when it becomes reality.

To assume that the masses will remain for ever in this trap is the sum-total of all pessimisms, and explains why so many of our young artists get drunk or commit suicide or both.

Examine our society and inquire, what force in it has power, or is capable of developing power, to replace capitalism? There is only one possible answer: the organized workers, whom capitalism has herded into large-scale industry. To hold this belief does not mean to idealize our present labour unions, which are a product of the competitive system, and tarred with its brush. But one may make concerning the working masses two assertions: first, they constitute the principal element in our society which lives by production, rather than by the manipulation of prices; second, they can prevail by solidarity, and in no other way. So in the course of their struggle for power they are evolving a new and higher ideal, and constitute the germ of the new society, based upon brotherhood and co-operation. Thus, fundamentally, the ideals of revolutionary labour are identical with those of the vital creative artist; which is what this book set out to prove.

I am appealing to the young writer to cast away the old egocentric psychology of our predatory world. I say that the artist who becomes a caterer to classes and coteries condemns himself to narrowness, sterility, and decay. Those who serve our present luxury classes present themselves to my view as monkeys in a cage, having nothing to do but pick vermin from their hides, and invent and practise vices in public. This abhorrence which I voice may seem extreme, but it is mild compared to the storm of revolutionary feeling which will sweep them and their keepers away.

I plead with the young writer to identify himself with the real ideals of the awakening industrial democracy. I plead for labour; and perhaps you will argue, that is merely another class. But there is a fundamental difference—in that the advancing workers welcome all men and women to the ranks of workers, whereas the exploiters do everything to keep their power in their own hands, and to keep others beneath their feet. That is precisely the difference between a basis for true art, and a basis for false art. The revolutionary appeal may be summed up in these words—that the artist should produce warm-heartedly for the whole of mankind, instead of with greed and contempt for a greedy and contemptuous group.

The time has come when the issue can no longer be evaded; the era of social revolution is upon us, and if you are blind to its presence, or indifferent to its promise, you are less than a full-sized social mind. I plead with the young writer to pull off the blinders which ruling-class propaganda seeks to fasten over his eyes. Look at the modern world for yourself; study the class struggle, the key to the whole of our epoch; and speak for humanity, and for the future, not for parasites and plunderers, however beautifully decked out in conventions and sentimentalities of their own invention.

There is a happier day coming, when an enlightened community will foster vital art, and a writer may speak the truth without fear of boycott and extinction. I do not attempt to deal with that day, which seems far off and dim to our clouded vision. Ours is the time of pain and sacrifice, when the honest man's reward is the inner knowledge of a service rendered to the race. It is a time of knavery enthroned, and buncombe and triviality set up in the seats of glory. But the movement for social justice is organizing itself and acquiring power; it has its champions in every civilized land—including the greatest of artists; I think we shall not have to wait many decades in America for the coming of a literature based upon scientific optimism and constructive social vision.

INDEX

(Roman numerals refer to chapters, Arabic to pages)

I N D E X

[214]

INDEX